# LONELY PATH

A BODHI KING NOVEL

MELISSA F. MILLER

BROWN STREET BOOKS

Published by Brown Street Books.

Brown Street Books ISBN: 978-1-940759-32-6

# ALSO BY MELISSA F. MILLER

*The Sasha McCandless Legal Thriller Series*

Irreparable Harm

Inadvertent Disclosure

Irretrievably Broken

Indispensable Party

Lovers and Madmen (Novella)

Improper Influence

A Marriage of True Minds (Novella)

Irrevocable Trust

Irrefutable Evidence

A Mingled Yarn (Novella)

Informed Consent

International Incident

Imminent Peril

The Humble Salve (Novella)

*The Aroostine Higgins Novels*

Critical Vulnerability

Chilling Effect

Calculated Risk


*The Bodhi King Novels*

Dark Path

Lonely Path

Hidden Path


*The We Sisters Three Romantic Comedic Mysteries*

Rosemary's Gravy

Sage of Innocence

Thyme to Live

Lost and Gowned

*One whose mind*
*is enmeshed in sympathy*
*for friends and companions,*
*neglects the true goal.*
*Seeing this danger in intimacy,*
*wander alone(.)*

THE BUDDHA, SUTTA NIPATA

# CHAPTER ONE

*Smith House Parking Lot, Mount Royal Park,
Montreal, Quebec, Canada
Sunday, 30 minutes after sunset*

The student meandered his way down from the angel statue, still buzzing and mildly dazed from Tam-Tams. He'd eaten perhaps one too many space cakes and decided this was the time to try his first dose of Solo.

He'd heard the hippies at the drum circle talking about it, about how the drug was no fun because it didn't connect them to the Universe or make them feel part of the great cosmos. Instead it made a person feel contained and in control, powerful and self-possessed, with no need or desire to make any connections.

He wanted that feeling more than anything.

He lost his footing and stumbled onto the paved lot. Then he hesitated and looked around. Now what? He was only in his first year at university, and he had little experience in approaching dealers to buy drugs—or women to ask out, or professors to seek clarification about a lesson. Sweat beaded on his upper lip as he edged closer to the nearest loitering dealer.

The guy gave him a laconic once-over. "What you need, man?"

"Solo?" he squeaked. "Solo," he tried again in a stronger voice.

"You a cop?"

He shook his head rapidly. "No. I'm a student."

"Easy, man. I don't have it. You want some Molly? I got pure Molly, the real deal."

His friends had warned him not to buy Molly in the park—it was always cut with something, and sometimes had no MDMA in it at all. Better to get that on campus. "I want to try Solo."

"It's your life." The dealer made a clicking sound, like a disappointed mother, then jerked his head to his right. "You want to see Christian. The African in the yellow hat."

"Thanks."

He took a few steps away from the Molly dealer and toward Christian then stopped. His high from the weed was wearing off, and this whole idea seemed stupid. But if he didn't go through with the buy now, these guys might think he *was* a cop. They could jump him.

He lowered his head and hurried over to Christian before he lost his nerve. He waited, staring at the ground, while the man finished up a sale.

"You looking for something?" the dealer asked.

"Solo."

"You ever do Solo before?"

The student lifted his head in surprise at the question. "Uh ... no. Why?"

"This is serious stuff. You just starting out, maybe you want some pure weed, ganja?"

"I want Solo."

He realized that he really did. He wanted to know what it was like to feel powerful and alone instead of lonely.

Christian appraised him. "Man, it's your funeral. It's twenty a pill."

"One pill's all I need?" He dug a crumpled bill out of his jeans pocket.

"Yeah. And it's all I'm selling a virgin. You like it, you know where to find me." He replaced the twenty with a small square of aluminum foil wrapped around a single pill.

"Thanks."

The dealer turned away.

The student walked back toward the trail through the park to find a wide open space to take the pill. He sat down in the grass, unwrapped the tiny foil packet, and examined the bright purple tablet. He popped it into his mouth then lay on his back and looked up at the deepening night sky while he waited to feel different.

He didn't have to wait long.

A surge of power coursed through his body and he sat bolt upright. He stretched out his arms and stared at his fingertips. They tingled and pulsed with energy.

He stood and turned in a slow circle, taking in the trees and grass that surrounded him. He was a god. He was separate from it all, in control of everything. No, he *was* everything—a self-contained cosmos.

He was the hero in his own epic story. He tipped his head back and laughed.

The laugh froze in his throat. Caught there as his thrumming body numbed. Panic invaded his high. He couldn't move his fingers. He couldn't move his feet. His breath turned to cement in his lungs as he crumpled to the ground.

His brain received the last weak electrical impulses from his neurons and processed them into his final thought: The end.

# CHAPTER TWO

*Chateau Frontenac*
*Quebec City, Quebec, Canada,*
*Sunday night*

Bodhi King brought the rental car to a stop in front of the entrance to the iconic hotel. A smiling valet hurried over as Bodhi exited the car. Bodhi noted his name tag, which identified him as 'Timothy S.'

"Welcome to Quebec City." Timothy's pride was evident in his voice, as if he were personally responsible for the historic old city and its charms.

"Thank you." Bodhi shouldered his large backpack.

Then he stepped back to gaze up at the stately, castle-like structure. Its many copper turrets, peaks, and roofs gleamed in the night.

"Wow," he breathed.

He'd seen pictures, of course—who hadn't? The hotel even had an entry in *The Guinness Book of World Records* as the most-photographed hotel on the planet. But standing in front of it, seeing it in person, was staggering.

"She's a beauty, isn't she, Mr. ..." Timothy trailed off, waiting for him to supply a name.

"King. Bodhi King."

Recognition sparked in his eyes. "Ah, Dr. King, you're one of the speakers, yes? For the conference?"

Bodhi blinked. "Yes, I am."

The valet noted his surprise with a laugh. "The conference attendees will be most of the hotel guests later in the week—they've booked most of the rooms. But we were told that the speakers would begin to arrive today, and to make you feel most welcome."

"I see. Have any other speakers arrived?"

Guillaume Loomis, the programming coordinator for the meeting of the North American Society of Forensic Pathology, had encouraged him to come in a few days early to explore the city. The conference itself didn't begin until Wednesday, although Dr. Loomis had arranged for the panelists and presenters to meet informally on Monday and to attend a private session on Tuesday. Bodhi was hopeful he would be able to keep a low profile until the Monday luncheon.

"Some have. Mainly those of you with international flights and some of the speakers who live in distant provinces. Most people will check in tomorrow."

Perfect. His plan to walk the city in the morning should go off without a hitch.

"Great. Well, good night, Timothy." Bodhi handed over the keys to the subcompact and a folded bill.

The valet placed the latter in his pocket. *"Merci.* I'll have your bags sent up to your room."

"No need. I have everything right here." He patted the backpack.

"Very good, sir."

Bodhi took another look at the building's grand facade before walking into the lobby.

Inside, the tan marble floors, dark oak panels, and shimmering chandeliers set into the blue coffered ceiling matched the splendor and glamour of the exterior.

Only one reception desk was staffed at this late hour, and a woman was checking in. Bodhi stood a respectful distance away and took the opportunity to gaze at the carefully arranged art and antiques while he waited.

"Good night," the woman called to the man behind

the desk and she disappeared around a corner, clutching her room key.

Her lilting voice held a hint of a Southern accent. Something about her inflection was familiar. It stirred old memories that tried, but couldn't quite manage, to rise to the surface. Bodhi turned to get a glimpse of the speaker, but all he saw was the back of her head.

"Sir?" The registration clerk smiled at him.

"Oh, right. Hi." He put the woman's voice out of his mind and stepped up to the registration desk.

---

Eliza Rollins let herself into her room, switched on the lights, and dropped the key onto the desk. She crossed the room and swept the drapes open to reveal the historic city, agleam with lights.

She rested her forehead against the cool glass and looked out into the night. Quebec City was a far cry from Belle Rue, Louisiana. But at least the smattering of French she'd picked up during her years working in Creole country might come in handy.

She pulled out her mobile phone and found the icon for her contact list. She pressed 'CoP' to call the St. Mary's Parish Chief of Police.

"Chief Bolton," he answered formally in his gruff voice, even though she knew his phone would identify her as 'Doc R.'

"It's me, Fred."

"I know. How's Quebec City?"

She peered out the window. "It was dark when I got here, so I didn't see much. But this hotel is indescribable. I understand where it got its name. It truly looks like a castle."

"Yeah? Make sure you take some pictures. I doubt the Association of Small Town Chiefs will ever book one of our meetings there."

They both chuckled at the thought. It *was* almost unbelievable that she, the coroner of itty-bitty St. Mary's Parish, had been invited to present her paper at an international meeting of forensic pathologists. She'd pinched herself when Guillaume Loomis had called her.

"I miss you." The words flew out of her mouth unbidden.

"Ah, hell, I miss you, too, Eliza. But I couldn't very well leave Soldan in charge to go flitting off to Canada. The good people of St. Mary's Parish wouldn't be able to sleep at night."

She sighed. Fred's workaholic habits and his refusal to delegate made him a moderately bad boyfriend. Luckily for him, she was a socially awkward introvert who didn't like to go out to dinner—let alone travel internationally. But presenting her paper at this conference would be an honor, possibly the pinnacle of her career. She could hardly have refused. It sure would have been nice to have had him come along, though.

"I know. It's too bad. This place is so romantic." She sighed.

"Eliza ..."

"I know, you couldn't."

There was a heavy silence.

"Tell you what, we'll go to New Orleans for a long weekend next month. We'll eat some good food, listen to some jazz. You can pick the hotel—a haunted one, a romantic one, whatever you want. Okay?" He lowered his voice to a growl.

"Okay." Her mouth curved into a smile.

"You oughta draw yourself a bath, have a soak, and relax. Rest up. You're representing the great state of Louisiana, after all. You've gotta wow those Canucks."

"Good night, Fred."

"Good night, baby."

She ended the call and glanced at the thick packet of conference materials that had been delivered to her room along with her bag. For a moment, she considered reviewing the papers while in the bath, but Fred was right. As a lifelong introvert, she wasn't exactly relishing the next several days of socializing and public speaking. She'd be more effective if she was well rested and fresh.

The envelope could wait until the morning.

# CHAPTER THREE

*Sainte-Anne, Île d'Orléans*
*The Quebec countryside*

Virgil was leaving the plant when his cell phone vibrated in his pocket. He pulled the heavy wooden doors shut and juggled the phone and the key ring.

"Hello?" He squeezed the phone between his shoulder and his ear and jiggled the padlock into place.

A stream of accented garbled French and English hit his ears. The man was screaming.

"Stop. Breathe."

His caller did as instructed.

"Good. Now, who is this?" A great number of people had his telephone number, but he made it a point not to save any of their names as contacts. Why do the police's work for them?

"It's Christian, man." The cadence of his caller's voice had slowed, but he was still gulping for air.

African immigrant. One of the Mont Royal Park dealers. Decent producer.

"What's the problem?" Virgil frowned to himself as he crossed the courtyard from the crumbling building to the gate. He hoped Christian wasn't about to tell him about yet another sweep of the park. His lawyers would eventually secure the release of most of his dealers, but it would cost him time and money.

"Another dead white boy."

Virgil stopped in his tracks, just outside the entrance gate.

"Solo?" he asked, although he already knew the answer. He pulled the gate shut, turned the key, and tested the gate to ensure the lock was engaged.

"Yes. I sold him one hit. Just one. Then I damn near tripped over his body walking home. Just laying there in the grass, on the hill about fifty yards from the parking lot, eyes wide open."

"You're sure he's dead?"

"What am I—a doctor? He didn't have a pulse and wasn't breathing. What do you call that?"

Virgil ignored the question. "Is he still there?"

"Yeah. He's dead. He's not going anywhere."

"Take his identification out of his wallet and roll him into the bushes near the drinking fountain."

"What? No, man. I'm not—"

"Do as I say. Drop the ID into the Saint Lawrence on your way home."

A long pause, some indistinct mumbling. Then, "Fine. What about the rest of the wallet?"

"I don't care what you do as long as you're smart about it. Keep the cash, sell the cards."

He slid into the driver's seat, planning his next steps. If the buyer was dead, it was a simple matter to leave him in the park for the police to clean up. But on the off chance the man wasn't quite dead .... No, he had to confirm it for himself.

He gritted his teeth as he started the car. This detour would throw off his schedule.

"Hey, man? What's wrong with this stuff? You gotta stop selling it until you get it right." The dealer's voice shook.

Virgil laughed. "Ah, Christian—the drug dealer with a conscience. I'm sure the overdoses weigh heavily on you when you close your eyes to sleep. If it bothers you so much, find a priest and make a confession. I can stop supplying you at any time."

"No, no, that's not what I mean," Christian protested

right away. "Solo's pure gold, my best seller. Just ... why do people keep dying—are you cutting it with something nasty?"

"Rest assured my drugs are pure. I don't 'cut' them with anything." He bristled at the idea.

The unique flood of energy and rush of adrenaline that Solo provided were the result of a carefully calibrated cocktail of chemicals that Virgil had spent years perfecting. He tried to hit that sweet spot—the mixture that would deliver an intense, addictive high without causing paralysis and brain death. Most times, he succeeded. But the delicate interplay of neurochemical responses varied from person to person and were less precise than his dosages.

That said, he didn't need to explain himself to a street dealer. He ended the call and pulled out onto the winding road.

H e returned several hours later in the middle of the night.

A ragged moan rose from the back seat as he parked the car. He tilted the rearview mirror to examine his passenger. Christian's latest overdose had rolled from the bench seat to the floor of the car. He glanced up and down the deserted road then hurried to unlock the gate before dealing with the college student in the car.

Contrary to Christian's report, the man—although in fairness he was hardly more than a boy; nineteen at the most, Virgil guessed—had not been dead when Virgil arrived at the park and found him in the bushes. He had been in the same state as the others. Paralyzed, catatonic, barely breathing. But alive. Which meant Virgil couldn't risk leaving him in Mont Royal Park. He'd have to be dealt with, like the others.

He walked around to the rear driver's door and heaved the man out on to the ground. Then he arranged the man's arms around his own shoulders and dragged him up the pathway in near total darkness. The man was dead weight, and Virgil was breathing heavily.

When they reached the rotting porch, he propped the man against the railing and caught his breath. Then he unlocked the door and hauled the man into the dark front parlor to the right of the hallway. Then he had to sit for a few minutes before he returned to the front door. He made a note to find the time to get back to the gym; his burning lungs and ragged breathing were evidence that he'd been spending too much time in the lab and not enough on the treadmill.

He secured the door. Then, leaving the man where

he rested on the parlor floor, he turned to the left and walked down the narrow passageway that led to the laboratory and packaging rooms.

# CHAPTER FOUR

*Chateau Frontenac*
*Monday morning*

Bodhi finished his tea then turned his attention to the packet of conference materials he'd been too tired to read after settling into his room the previous night. The first item on the agenda was a meet and greet for each of the panels.

It made sense. In his admittedly limited experience, conference organizers rarely scheduled such introductory get togethers, but when they did, the panels invariably ran more smoothly.

He paged through the schedule until he found his panel, "Forensic Black Swans—When the Pathologist

Confronts the Unimaginable." He read through the list of panelists, noting with interest the titles of their various papers.

In addition to his own piece, "Scared to Death: When Beliefs Kill," his fellow panel members were presenting on topics as diverse as "Chimerism: The Case of the Twice-Dead Man," "The MacGyver Technique: Getting a Fingerprint from Peeled Skin Using Disposable Gloves and Scotch Tape," and "Plucked: When Traditional Tribal Death Rituals Collide with Modern Time-of-Death Determinations."

His eyes drifted back to the name of the author of the tribal death ritual paper—Eliza G. Rollins, M.D., St. Mary's Parish Coroner, Belle Rue, Louisiana—and his pulse quickened. Oddly enough, he'd had a medical school classmate named Eliza Rollins.

Could this Eliza Rollins be *his* Eliza Rollins?

*C'mon, Bodhi,* he admonished himself. *Neither the first name nor the last name was that unusual. Besides, the last he'd heard, Eliza'd moved to Texas to do her residency. Just a coincidence.*

He supposed he could confirm that it wasn't the same Eliza Rollins by flipping to the speakers' biographies printed at the end of the conference programming guide. But he didn't.

Instead, he poured a second cup of tea and consulted

his walking map of Quebec City. It made sense to save the winding streets of Old Quebec's upper and lower towns for tomorrow, when it seemed he'd have more free time.

But, judging from the map, he would definitely be able to walk along Terrasse Dufferin then visit Battle-fields Park, with its famed Plains of Abraham, this morning. If he left now he might even sneak in some time at the national art museum before the first scheduled activity of the day.

With the promise of the famed art gallery spurring him on, he refolded his map and tucked it into his back pocket, rinsed his mug at the bathroom sink, and grabbed his wallet and cell phone from the desk.

---

E liza closed her eyes and slumped against the cool bathroom wall and felt her heart thump wildly in her chest. Her entire body trembled. She began to pant—rapid, shallow gasps for air—and then the sweating started.

She forced herself to take a deep breath, letting the air fill her lungs and belly for a slow count of *one, two, three, four*. She exhaled for a seven count.

The adrenaline was still flooding her system.

She repeated the slow deep intake and release of breath. Again. And again.

"You're not really dying. You're not having a heart attack. You're having a panic attack. You are not dying." She said the words in a firm voice. They echoed off the marble walls.

She dug her fingernails into her palms and pressed the soles of her feet hard into the floor. By grounding herself in the real world, she would fight off the perceived danger.

As her breathing became more rhythmic, her heartbeat slowed and she stopped shaking. Spent, she closed her eyes and spoke out loud again.

This time, her voice was kind and soothing, as if she were talking to a frightened child. "You're okay, Eliza. You're just scared. It's okay to be scared."

She sat on her bathroom floor for what seemed to be a very long time, breathing and telling herself she was all right. When her dried sweat made her shiver, she slowly stood and poured herself a glass of water from the sink.

She leaned against the vanity and sipped the water, staring at her reflection in the mirror as she drank. Her hair was lank from perspiration. Her face was drained of color. She did not look like a woman who was ready to face a room full of strangers ... and the man who'd been her lover umpteen years ago.

Her eyes fell to the floor, where the list of panelists that had triggered her panic attack lay crumpled against the door.

*Bodhi King.*

The name conjured up a generous smile, warm eyes, and hands that explored her body in a leisurely way, like their owner had all the time in the world to learn every inch of her. And back then, she believed he did.

Her hands began to tremble again.

"No. Stop." She leveled her gaze at her reflection. "You're going to pull yourself together, Eliza. You're better than this."

She turned and opened her toiletry bag. She found her lavender essential oils and turned the faucets to fill the bath with warm water.

While the tub filled, she closed her eyes and imagined herself walking calmly into the meeting room. She would smile at the other presenters. Avoid Bodhi, if at all possible. Focus on her paper. And survive the next three and a half days.

# CHAPTER FIVE

**B**odhi returned from his sightseeing at the last possible moment, having made it to exactly one of the spots on his itinerary.

After strolling along the Dufferin Terrace, he'd found himself in Montmorency Park. He'd planned to walk through it quickly, but between the striking views of the Saint Lawrence River from the ramparts, the old cannons, the statues and the still, silent weight of history that hung on the air, he'd lost track of time.

Stepping into the lobby of the hotel jarred him back into the present. The low hum of lively voices replaced the ghosts of soldiers and farmers, pioneers and artists. He checked the time and hurried toward the elevator.

Guillaume Loomis emerged from a clutch of suit-wearing men and snagged him by the elbow.

"Ah, Dr. King, right on time!" He began to steer Bodhi toward the cluster of men.

Bodhi sneaked another glance at his watch. "Actually, Dr. Loomis, don't I have a few minutes before the session begins? I was out walking around your beautiful city, taking in some of the sights. I just need to change my clothes and grab my name badge."

"Nonsense." Guillaume tightened his grip. "We're breaking into small groups. I'm sure your fellow panelists will be able to remember your name, and your attire is just fine. Just fine."

Bodhi eyed Guillaume's tan suit then let his gaze travel to his own outfit—brown cargo pants and a green and white striped shirt. Guillaume watched him placidly.

"Really, we know our American neighbors are more casual," the Canadian assured him.

"Okay, as long as it's fine with you." Bodhi had no intention of arguing his way into a suit and tie. In fact, he'd had a devil of a time finding his dress shoes to pack because it had been so long since he'd last worn business attire.

"Quite fine."

As they approached the assembled group, an elevator bell dinged. Bodhi turned toward the sound as the doors parted. Eliza Rollins stepped off the elevator and scanned the lobby.

Even though he hadn't seen her in thirteen years, he would have recognized her anywhere. She looked exactly as he remembered her.

"Eliza," he called.

Guillaume turned and waved. "Ah, you know Dr. Rollins?"

"We were medical school classmates."

Eliza's clear brown eyes met his and, for a moment, her smile faltered. Then she blinked and crossed the lobby to join them.

"I understand there's no need for introductions. Why don't I let the two of you catch up for a minute? How lucky that you're on the same panel." He consulted his watch. "Your group is lunching in the Petit Frontenac Room."

He pointed vaguely down the hallway before making his way back to the waiting panelists to sort them into their various small groups.

"How lucky," Eliza echoed the organizer's words in a dry tone.

Bodhi searched her face and realized she didn't share his joy at their chance meeting.

He flashed back to April 2004.

It was two weeks after Match Day, when medical

students learned where they'd be completing their residencies. Eliza had matched with the University of Texas's pathology residence program and would begin her studies in July. He'd gotten a spot in the University of Pittsburgh Medical Center's pathology program and would do his residency in his home medical school—an unusual but welcome occurrence.

As they walked along Forbes Avenue, headed for the Chinese restaurant she liked, she'd been light-hearted and chatty, mostly about her upcoming visit to Dallas to find an apartment.

"Since you matched here and you don't have to move, you can come out and help me get settled. We'll find a new favorite restaurant."

She smiled up at him and a worry that had been floating in and out of his mind ever since Match Day rematerialized.

He stopped walking and guided her out of the flow of pedestrian traffic. Then he said, "We need to focus on our residencies. There's a lot at stake. After graduation, I think we both need to move on."

She blinked at him. "Move on? Are you breaking up with me?"

"It's not you. It's just that this attachment's not healthy—for either of us. All of life is a solitary journey, Eliza, we can't—"

"Spare me the Buddhist bullshit."

She shook his hand off her arm and refused to listen to any further explanation. Then she'd said she had a headache and didn't feel like having dinner after all.

Over the next month, he'd tried to talk to her, but she kept blowing him off. It was a busy time of year for everyone—completing their requirements, preparing for their residencies. The next thing he knew, they were graduating. A few weeks later, she was in Dallas, and he was starting his orientation.

He'd never had the chance to explain himself. Or apologize.

Now, standing in the elegant reception space of one of the world's most romantic, iconic hotels and looking into the eyes of the only woman he'd ever loved, a deep sense of shame washed over him. He accepted it, allowing the feeling to settle in his bones.

"Eliza—"

"Don't. Please, don't. Whatever it is you're going to say, don't say it. Let's just go join the others and get this over with." Her voice was low but steady. Her clear brown eyes pleaded with him.

He was quiet for a moment, noting the slight tremor in her hands.

"I can't wait to hear about your paper. The death

rituals of traditional cultures have always been of interest to me," he said finally.

She let out a relieved sigh. "I think the Petit Frontenac Room is over here."

She flashed him a smile that didn't reach her eyes and began to walk along the corridor.

## CHAPTER SIX

Seeing Bodhi wasn't as painful as she'd thought it would be. This realization hit Eliza with full force while Dr. Bechtel, the cheerful pathology program director from the McAllen University Hospital Centre, was explaining how he planned to moderate their panel.

She leaned back in her chair and looked through the wall of windows at the view of the river while she considered this surprising development.

*Perhaps time does heal all wounds. Or, perhaps, a certain gruff but charming small-town chief of police had healed her wounds.*

She craned her neck around Dr. Malvern and risked a glance at Bodhi. He sat two chairs away, leaning forward and listening intently. She could see the faintest hint of the intense student he'd been when they'd dated underneath his Zen-like calm and deliberateness. He twirled a pencil between his long, thin fingers—classic surgeon's fingers—as he nodded along to Dr. Bechtel's words.

Bodhi must have felt her watching him because he turned his head toward her and locked eyes with her. She was about to look away when he flashed her a grin.

Flustered, she dropped her gaze to her lap.

"Would that be agreeable to you, Dr. Rollins?" Dr. Bechtel asked.

She snapped her head up. "Oh. I ... certainly." She stammered her answer and immediately wondered what she'd just signed up for.

He smiled. "Wonderful. I know some speakers don't like going first, but you *are* our only female presenter. I didn't want to appear discourteous."

*Crud. Well, at least she'd get it over with at the very beginning.*

"After Dr. Rollins has talked to the room about the Atchafalayan death rituals, let's move on to Dr. King and his voodoo deaths, then Dr. Ripple's unusual finger-printing technique, and, lastly, Dr. Malvern, who may have to join us to talk about chimerism once the panel has already begun. Is that right, Jon?"

Jon Malvern, a forensic biologist with the Provincial Forensic Laboratory and an adjunct professor at the

University of Montreal in the area of cellular biology and pathology, waved his hands in an apologetic gesture.

"Yes, I'm afraid I may. It's all hands on deck at the office with all these overdoses." He turned to Eliza on his left then to Bodhi on his right and explained, "The entire province is struggling with a rash of drug overdoses. It's quite sad."

"Not just Quebec," Dr. Ripple chimed in. "Ontario is also getting hit hard—Toronto, in particular. There's a brand new designer drug out there, and we don't know what it is. The toxicology reports are baffling."

Bodhi made an understanding noise. Eliza imagined he would have more experience with synthetic street drugs, having worked in a major city. The last drug death she'd handled in Belle Rue had been the result of an unfortunate printing error on the dosing instructions for Effie LaForge's chemotherapy pills.

"Not to worry," Dr. Bechtel assured him. "So, after Jon's presented, we'll open the floor for questions."

"Will you ask the audience members to direct their questions to a specific person or may we decide amongst ourselves who's best suited to answer it?" Dr. Ripple asked.

"I think the latter, Claude. And if more than one of you would like to respond, that's also fine. I may even chime in from time to time myself."

Eliza felt her attention drifting again. One of the benefits of her situation was that she rarely had to sit through administrative meetings of this sort. She stifled a yawn.

Felix Bechtel showed no signs that he was ready to wrap up the world's most boring meet and greet.

She shifted in her seat. Held back another yawn. Finally, she turned her attention to the remnants of her boxed lunch.

She was chasing a grape around the container with her spoon when a shadow fell across the table. She lifted her head and spotted an amused-looking Bodhi standing a foot or so away.

"Felix said we're free to go."

Jon and Claude were already hurrying out of the room with Felix at their side.

"Oh. I guess my mind must have wandered."

"I guess so."

She gathered up her boxed lunch container and napkins then looked around for a tray or trash can.

"Felix said to just leave them," Bodhi told her.

"Oh. I hate not cleaning up after myself."

He nodded. "It feels wrong, doesn't it?"

"It does."

"Eliza, something else that feels wrong is how we left

things—how I left things between us. Please let me buy you an early dinner." His voice was low, serious.

"I don't think that's a good idea."

"Why not?"

"Well, for one thing we just ate lunch." She cringed at how silly it sounded. While it was a true fact, it wasn't her actual objection.

"I have a rental car. I'm going to explore Île d'Orléans. There's a park with a waterfall that's wider than Niagara Falls, and a string of farming villages. A chocolate shop. A cheese shop that sells the oldest style of cheese in North America. It'd be nice to have your company."

She gnawed on her lower lip, trying to decide how to say what she was about to say. "It sounds like fun. But ... I'm seeing someone."

He looked at her blankly for a moment. "Today? You have a friend in town?"

"No. I mean I'm dating someone—back home."

Understanding bloomed on his face. "I see. I promise my intentions are honorable."

She gave him a close look. They'd always enjoyed exploring Pittsburgh's hidden nooks and crannies and overlooked neighborhoods during their limited free time back in medical school. And wandering around the countryside sounded more appealing than holing up in her room and worrying about her upcoming public speaking role.

"I don't know—"

"I'd like to spend some time with you, Eliza. As an old friend, nothing more."

"Tell me more about this cheese."

"It's called *paillasson*. It's buttery and served grilled or fried or something. And the only place you can get it is at this one cheese shop on the island. How could you pass that up?"

She had to admit she probably couldn't, but she didn't tell him that yet. Instead, she said, *"Paillasson? Doesn't that mean doormat?"*

A wide grin broke across his face. "I think so. Don't you want to know the story behind it?"

She tilted her head from side to side, weighing her answer. "I actually really do."

He laughed. "It's settled then. Meet you in the lobby in an hour?"

She took a moment to check in with herself. Her breathing was measured. Her heart rate was normal. Her hands were steady. She nodded. "See you then."

## CHAPTER SEVEN

*Provincial Forensic Laboratory*
*Montreal, Quebec*
*Monday afternoon*

J on Malvern hustled into his office and grabbed his lab coat from the hook on the back of the door. He hadn't yet buttoned it when Lucy Kim, the senior toxicologist, knocked on his door and pushed it open.

"Oh, good, you're back." She managed a harassed-looking smile.

"Traffic was bad or I'd have been here sooner. What'd I miss?"

"More of the same. I got the STAs on four more overdoses."

He shook his head. The STAs—or systemic toxicological analyses—that Lucy was running were comprehensive, state-of-the-art tests. Her team had been testing the urine, blood, and hair samples of the overdose victims for every known street and prescription drug and coming up empty. Whatever was killing these people was a completely new concoction, a chemical cipher that neither enzyme-linked immunoassay, gas chromatography/mass spectrometry, nor any of Lucy's other tests could decode.

That was the problem with designer drugs. The black market chemists who created them stayed a step ahead of the authorities by intentionally tweaking the components. And even when the recipe wasn't being altered by design, because illicit drug labs lacked quality assurance or standardization procedures, ingredients and amounts could fluctuate wildly from one batch to the next. It made identification a nightmare.

Although Jon wasn't a toxicologist, there was ample cross-over between his specialty and hers. And they both knew the value of looking outside one's area of expertise, especially when faced with a road block like this one. He wracked his brain trying to coming up with a novel next step.

"Do you want to try analyzing bone marrow?" he ventured.

"Maybe, eventually. I actually stopped by because I have an idea, but I need your help."

"Say the word."

"Thanks. I'd like you to culture some glial cells from the brain matter samples for me."

He blinked.

The glia were the neurons' often overlooked, but crucial and multifunctional partner. For decades, neuroscientists focused on the neurons and believed the abundant glial cells were unimportant. In reality, they played several critical roles that keep the central nervous system running. Glial cells built and pruned synapses, formed myelin to insulate neurons, enabled communication between neurons and synapses, and were involved in learning and creativity. In short, they were wonderfully diverse. But he wasn't sure where she was going with this.

"What are you thinking?" he asked.

Lucy made a clicking sound with her tongue. "I'm not sure, Jon. I just keep thinking if there's a new neurotoxin out there—or a slightly tweaked one that the tests aren't picking up—we might find evidence of glial cell destruction or mutation, particularly in the microglia."

He nodded excitedly. It was a novel approach, but it was sensible. The microglial cells functioned as the brain's immune system. Recent research had implicated chronic microglial activation and inflammation in a number of neurodegenerative diseases. If the synthetic drug they were dealing with was a neurotoxin, it was possible that it would damage the same pathways as the neurodegenerative diseases.

After a moment, he tempered his enthusiasm and slid into the role of devil's advocate. It was his duty, as both a colleague and a friend, to poke holes in her hypothesis.

"We're starting from an assumption that this drug, whatever it is, crosses the blood-brain barrier?"

"Most addictive drugs do. And I think it's safe to say our mystery drug is addictive, don't you?"

He shrugged. "Probably."

"I know it's a long shot, but I have to do *something*." Her frustration took physical form. She stiffened her spine and clenched her jaw.

"Why don't I prepare both—neuronal and glial cultures? You can run whatever assays you can think of to measure cell death, and I'll see what I can come up with to identify demylenation, inflammation, and deterioration."

Her face eased into a grin. "You're a gem, Jon. A total gem."

## CHAPTER EIGHT

*The road outside Sainte-Anne, Île d'Orléans*

Bodhi glanced at Eliza. She had settled into the rental car's passenger seat with a blissful sigh after they'd left the restaurant.

"Who'd ever imagine a restaurant menu built entirely around black currants?" she asked when she caught his eye.

"It was unique," he agreed. The *cassis*, or black currant, farm and restaurant was only one of the charmingly unusual points of interest they'd encountered on the small island.

After tromping across a suspension bridge at Montmorency Falls Park and marveling at the thrill-seeking zip liners, they'd stopped at the cheese shop so Eliza could taste the *paillasson,* served up by an enthusiastic cheese merchant dressed in seventeenth-century garb.

Bodhi had found the story about the cheese delightful. Eliza had found the actual cheese less so. "I think I know why they call it doormat. It tastes like feet," she'd whispered as they'd left the building.

He'd made up for the cheese with the promised stop at the chocolatier. Followed by a vineyard. And a produce stand. Their gustatory tour of the island culminated with a meal of black currant-sauced duck confit for her and black currant, mushroom and onion confit for him, black currant wine and lemonade, and black currant sorbet.

Watching Eliza eat and drink her way through Île d'Orléans was a treat in itself. She peppered the shop proprietors with questions and reacted with delight and surprise at each new treat, even the cheese. Spending the afternoon with her brought memories of their heady medical school romance rushing back to him.

He let the easy companionability of the last several hours wash over him as the sun sank below the horizon and he pointed the car back to Quebec City.

After several moments of contented silence, Eliza suddenly said, "Why did you break up with me, Bodhi?"

Her voice was neutral, but he noticed how she

tensed her body and wrapped her arms around her midsection.

He was silent for a moment as he formulated a response. He owed her complete honesty, but he wanted to take care not to cause her new pain.

Finally, he said, "I made a careless mistake. I was scared. We were both moving on to the next phase in our medical careers and I believed that the Buddha's teachings on attachment meant that I should enter that phase alone. I was wrong, as it turns out. But I panicked. And I've regretted it ever since."

He let his eyes drift away from the empty rural road and meet hers.

"Oh."

Neither of them spoke for a bit. Then he said, "And I was confused about the precept on sexual relationships."

He waited to see if she squirmed. He didn't want to elaborate if doing so would cause her discomfort. The last thing he wanted to do was to hurt her anew.

"What's the precept say?" she asked, keeping her eyes fixed on the road ahead.

"To refrain from committing sexual misconduct. The precept encourages us to cultivate and encourage open and honest relationships."

"That seems as if it would be doable without dumping your partner."

He winced. "I may have been a bit militant in my interpretation, Eliza. I knew that the monks were celibate in an effort to devote themselves to their studies of Buddhism. I thought I needed to be celibate, too, so I could devote myself to the practice of medicine. I was wrong." He tried to deliver the explanation without a whiff of excuse or self-pity.

She hugged her knees to her chest. Without taking her eyes off the road, she asked, "How long were you ... celibate—after me?"

His mind flashed to the women who'd briefly enticed his imagination but then had flitted out of his consciousness.

"I still am."

His answer seemed to suck the air out of the car. A haze of regret for his candor began to envelope him. Then suddenly, she gripped his arm.

"Bodhi! Stop the car!"

He jammed on the brakes, a reaction to the panic in her voice. The car squealed to a stop.

She kept a firm grasp on his upper arm and pointed to the right shoulder of the road. A very young woman, pale-faced and frozen, stood barefoot in the gravel.

He eased the car off the road and killed the engine.

"Look at her eyes," he murmured.

"I think she's in shock. I'll go to her first. Give me a few minutes to talk to her."

He nodded. Eliza had a calming way about her. Her decision to pursue pathology had always puzzled him. He understood she was introverted and shy, but her soothing, empathetic nature was a gift that was wasted on the dead. A live, distressed woman would find her manner comforting.

His own affinity for pathology was much more understandable. He did not fear death. He accepted and respected it. And he wanted to help the dead tell their stories.

He watched as she exited the car and slowly approached the woman. She stooped so that she was at eye level with the shorter woman before she spoke. After several minutes, she turned and gestured for him to join them.

As he crunched across the gravel, Eliza faced him.

"She's in shock," she said in a low voice.

He noted the woman's slack expression and wide, dilated eyes. She didn't track his approach. Rather, she kept her unblinking and blank eyes on Eliza.

"I'm Dr. King." He announced himself in a low, slow voice.

The woman didn't respond. He took in her filthy

dress and apron. Her mud-coated feet and the blood that had been trickling down her legs in fine lines and then dried, as if she'd marched through brambles some time ago. She didn't tremble or shiver. She stood, rigid and straight, and stared at Eliza.

"What's your name?" he tried.

No reaction.

After a moment, he said, *"Je m'appelle Docteur King. Elle est Docteure Rollins. Comment vous appelez-vous?"*

After a delay, the woman shifted her gaze and locked her eyes on his, although he could see no life behind them.

"Tatiana," she croaked in a slow voice that creaked like an unoiled door. *"Je m'appelle Tatiana."*

Bodhi called Guillaume, who patched him through to the Quebec City police, while Eliza performed a rudimentary exam on Tatiana in the backseat of the car. After saying her name, Tatiana had lapsed back into silence and didn't seem to register Eliza's touch as she checked her vitals and reflexes.

Bodhi explained the situation to the police then twisted around to talk to Eliza and Tatiana.

"Because you can't tell us where you're from or how you got here, we're going to take you to Quebec City. The authorities will help you."

Tatiana looked forward blankly.

"Say it in French," Eliza suggested.

Bodhi gestured in frustration. "My French is pretty rusty. What's your name is about the best I can do."

Eliza flashed him a half-smile. She turned to Tatiana and repeated his words in impeccable rapid-fire French. He'd forgotten Eliza lived in Cajun country.

He watched intently for the woman's reaction. If he hadn't been looking for it, he would have missed it. At the mention of the *service du police*, a light flickered in Tatiana's eyes. But she didn't speak. Or nod. Or otherwise acknowledge them.

"Go ahead," Eliza told him. "Take us to the station. I'll sit back here and keep Tatiana company." She picked up the woman's limp hand and clasped it between her own hands as he turned the key in the ignition and the car rumbled to life.

## CHAPTER NINE

Eliza crawled between the buttery high-thread count sheets and pulled the blanket up to her chin. She was bone weary and drained. The initial adrenaline spike from finding Tatiana had dissipated before they'd reached the police station.

Then the long hours of bright lights, bad coffee, and repeated questions and forms had flattened what was left of her spirit. By the time they'd left Tatiana in the care of a social worker, a victim's advocate, and a crisis counselor, Eliza could barely keep her eyes open.

Bodhi had guided her to the car as if she were a child or an invalid. She hadn't had the energy to protest.

She turned out the light and surrendered to a heavy sleep.

A ringing phone jarred her awake. She fumbled with

the light and then squinted at her phone's display. Fred was calling.

"Hello?" she croaked, her mouth cottony from sleep and acidic from the cassis wine.

"Were you sleeping, Liza Bean?"

"Mm, yeah. It's okay, though." She suddenly wanted to talk to Fred more than she wanted to rest. She pushed herself up on to her elbows.

"What time is it there? It's only eight-thirty here."

She squinted at the clock. "Nine-thirty."

"Shouldn't you be out hobnobbing with the other docs?" He laughed.

"It was a long day. Do you have time to talk?"

"Course I do. That's why I called you."

"Okay. First, I had a panic attack because—"

"Are you all right?" He cut her off in an urgent voice.

Fred had been witness to one of her attacks for the first time just months ago, right before she was to testify at an inquest. It had terrified him so much that his worry had forced her out of her own hysteria.

"I'm fine. I got a handle on it early. But the reason it happened was ..." she trailed off, searching for the right way to explain Bodhi to Fred.

"I know, babe. You were anxious about meeting all those other doctors, weren't you?"

"I was, but that's not why. I ... I know one of the

other panelists."

"You do? That's good, isn't it? Having a familiar face on your panel should make you feel more comfortable."

"Not exactly. His name is Bodhi King. He was my boyfriend when I was in medical school."

"Oh."

"He was the last man I dated seriously before you, Fred."

She waited. She and Fred had never discussed their dating histories. She figured that they both realized she hadn't reached her late thirties and he hadn't reached his late forties without some stops along the way.

Finally, he said haltingly, "Well, shoot, Eliza. Are you trying to tell me you're hung up on this guy?"

"No. I'm not. He broke my heart, that's the truth. But you mended it. That's also the truth."

A small *ahh* of relief sounded in her ear.

"Happy to be of service, ma'am."

His jokey police officer voice brought Tatiana rushing back to her. "But something terrible happened today. We went sightseeing on this island right outside the city, and on the way back we found a woman."

"You found a woman? Do you mean a body? Was she dead?"

"She wasn't dead. But I'm not sure I could fairly call her alive either. She was just standing on the side of the road. We thought she was in shock at first, but I don't know. She seemed … empty. She only spoke once. She said her name is Tatiana."

"Man, I'm sorry, sweetheart. That must've been rough."

"It was. But rougher for her. We took her to the police station. There's a whole team working to help her. And I think they're having her admitted to the hospital for observation. But I just can't get her out of my mind. I don't know if she has amnesia or locked in syndrome or she's traumatized, but she's not whole. And it's haunting me." She took a shuddering breath.

"Hey, hey. You helped her, Liza Bean. You and your friend did what you could do. The police up there in Quebec City are top notch. They'll take care of her."

His words swept over her like a balm, and the guilt and helplessness she felt over the sad young woman eased.

"I love you, Fred."

"I love you, too. Now you go back to sleep. A good night's rest'll do wonders for you."

She murmured a goodbye and turned out the light. He was right. She needed to regroup and recharge. As she closed her eyes, she reminded herself that Tatiana was in good hands and that the authorities were best positioned to help her.

# CHAPTER TEN

*Tuesday morning*

From his window, Bodhi watched the early morning joggers zoom back and forth across Dufferin Terrace like so many busy, colorful ants. Further out, on the river, ships glided through the water.

As Quebec City woke up and began the business of commerce, education, and living, he turned to his map to plot out his walking itinerary through the Upper and Lower Towns.

*Should he invite Eliza to join him?*

The question had surfaced in his mind several times since he'd awoken. He enjoyed her company. And their encounter with Tatiana had left him feeling unsettled. He didn't really want to be alone.

This urge for companionship was unfamiliar, so he inspected the feeling. Did he want company or did he want Eliza's company? He couldn't quite tell. Maybe he wanted both.

His cell phone rang, interrupting his thoughts.

"Hello?"

"Dr. King?"

"Yes."

"This is Inspector Commaire with the Quebec City Police Service. I trust I didn't wake you?" The inspector's English held just the faintest trace of a French accent.

"No, not at all. I was up. Are you calling about Tatiana?"

"Yes, I am."

"How's she doing today?" He was eager for an update as to her status. She hadn't been communicative when he and Eliza had left her the previous night, and her pale drawn face had stayed in his mind.

"I am afraid she's still not speaking. The doctors are running tests. We have run some tests of our own, which is why I'm calling."

"Oh?"

"Yes. Dr. Loomis suggested we reach out to you and Dr. Rollins for some assistance."

"Guillaume Loomis?"

"Correct. Dr. Loomis consults on problematic cases with our coroner, so he's been called in and believes we should also seek help from you and Dr. Rollins."

Bodhi wrinkled his forehead as he strained to make sense of the request. "I'm not sure how we can help you, inspector. We're trained to deal with dead people."

"Ah, yes, I realize this. According to our records, the woman you brought in last night is Tatiana Georgette Viant. And she is very much dead."

---

"I don't understand. Tatiana's not dead." Eliza repeated the statement for a third time.

Bodhi glanced at her for a second before turning his attention back to the traffic.

"Inspector Commaire said Guillaume would fill us in when we got there. I'm sure it's a case of mistaken identity." He spoke in a deliberately soothing tone in an effort to ease her mounting worry.

"I suppose." She bit down on her thumbnail. After a moment, she went on. "I mean, you must be right. No other explanation makes any sense."

"Right. And although his English was very good, I'm sure he's more comfortable speaking French. Maybe there was a vocabulary issue and he worded things less accurately than he'd intended."

"Maybe."

He returned his focus to navigating through the narrow streets, and she returned hers to gnawing on her thumbnail.

He knew they were both troubled by the same aspect of the strange call—if Tatiana Viant had been misidentified as a dead woman, once that error had been established, the case would have remained an investigation involving a living person. Why was the coroner's office involved at all?

## CHAPTER ELEVEN

"Tatiana Viant was declared brain dead eight months ago," Guillaume explained. He pushed a folder across the table toward Bodhi and Eliza.

Eliza flipped it open, and Bodhi leaned over to read the summary sheet clipped to the inside cover.

After they scanned the report, Guillaume continued, "She was a twenty-year-old history major at McAllen University in Montreal. Her roommate returned from the gym and found her lying on the floor beside her bed, breathing but nonresponsive. She was rushed to the McAllen University Health Centre."

Bodhi looked up. "Isn't that where Felix Bechtel works?"

"Yes, pathology is the quintessential small world,

isn't it? Unfortunately, Felix isn't aware of her case because his department didn't handle it."

That struck Bodhi as odd, but he didn't want to interrupt Guillaume's recitation.

"According to the report, she was comatose and paralyzed when she was admitted."

"Deep coma?" Eliza asked.

Guillaume nodded. "She presented with fixed nonreactive pupils and apnea. There was no evidence of brain stem reflex."

*Coma, apnea, and absence of brain stem reflexes. That generally meant brain death.* Bodhi could see the others drawing the same conclusion.

"When she was brought in, did she meet the Canadian criteria for a neurological determination of death?" Eliza asked.

"Not initially. When she arrived, she was still breathing, slowly and in a labored fashion—but she was breathing. During the intake assessment, however, all respiratory function ceased. She was placed on a ventilator so the medical team could investigate whether there were any confounding factors to explain her condition before making the official NDD."

"I assume they found no such factors?" Bodhi asked.

Guillaume pulled a face. "They never had the chance. Her parents arranged for her to be transported to their local hospital in Port Grey, Ontario, about a half hour outside Ottawa. That's where the determination of brain death was made. She was removed from the ventilator the next day and was buried in the family plot."

His words landed with a thud.

"How did the police come to the conclusion that the woman we found was Tatiana Viant? Beyond telling us her first name she didn't say anything. And she wasn't carrying any identification," Bodhi pointed out.

"One of the social workers who went with her to the hospital recognized her. Until quite recently, he had worked at McAllen's counseling center, and he ran grief counseling sessions for Tatiana's roommate and friends after her death. He'd seen many pictures of her."

Eliza shook her head. "This is obviously a bizarre coincidence. This woman may not even really be named Tatiana. But if she is, this is a simple mix-up. She resembles a dead woman."

"We emailed a picture of the woman calling herself Tatiana to the hospital in Ontario and to the Port Grey Police Department. They both insist the woman you found is Tatiana Viant. It's a difficult situation to be sure, but the police there contacted Mr. and Mrs. Viant and showed them the picture. They believe she's their daughter. The Viants are on their way in to see this woman and to submit DNA samples for testing."

The unnecessary heartbreak of creating false hope in grieving parents made Bodhi's stomach seize. Judging by Eliza's pained expression, she felt the same way.

"Guillaume, this is ludicrous. Tatiana Viant was buried." Eliza's voice was strained and shaky.

"A casket was buried. The Viants agreed to have it exhumed."

"Are you going to tell us it was empty?" she demanded.

"No, Dr. Rollins. It wasn't empty. It was filled with sandbags."

# CHAPTER TWELVE

S he was gone. She was really gone. Virgil dodged the vacant-eyed, mumbling workers who trudged, stiff-legged, from the lab to the packaging room, carrying trays of pills in their outstretched hands.

*Gone.*

His heart pounded. He ran back to the front of the house and retraced his steps.

*Think.*

She'd definitely been there when he'd stopped to check on production Sunday evening. He remembered that for a fact. When he walked into the room she'd briefly raised her head from the pill mould she was filling and it almost seemed as if she recognized him.

In the moment, he'd scoffed at himself for being ridiculous, a fool. She didn't have the cognitive capacity to know a person. She was no more than a rudimentary android. More of a robot or trained animal than a human being.

Now, he skidded through the halls shouting her name in the hope she might somehow know it and respond.

It was no use. She wasn't here.

But she had to be. Where else could she be? There was nowhere for her to go. And there was no way out. He was diligent about keeping the gate and the house locked up tight. He always followed the same routine. Always.

Unlock the entrance gate. Walk into the front yard and immediately lock the gate behind him. Unlock the front door. Let himself into the building and immediately lock the door behind him.

After he fed the workers and filled a suitcase with the bagged pills he made sure every door and window was secure before he left the house, locked it up, and then repeated the process with the gate before driving away.

Each step of the process was ingrained, always performed in the same order, never deviating.

He froze in horror as he remembered his return trip to Sainte-Anne, well after midnight, with the college student. He'd left the gate unlocked while he'd dragged the man into the house. And he was almost positive he'd left the door unlocked until he'd dumped his newest worker onto the parlor floor.

Could she have drifted out of the house and walked through the unlatched gate?

It seemed incredible to even consider. She hadn't been outside in eight months. She couldn't have formed the intention to go out. And there was no way she'd survive if she'd wandered off the property.

He grabbed the heavy-duty flashlight from the hook by the back door. He'd start in the basement and search every inch of the dilapidated structure. Then he'd comb the property and the surrounding woods.

If he didn't find her ... He couldn't even complete the thought. The consequences were beyond his imagination.

## CHAPTER THIRTEEN

After dropping the bombshell news about Tatiana Viant's casket, Guillaume walked Eliza and Bodhi through the warren of offices, introducing them to a cadre of busy employees who offered hurried greetings before returning to their work.

"Would you like a cup of coffee or tea?" he asked. "I've been remiss in offering."

"We had more pressing matters to discuss. But, now that you mention it, I really could use a coffee," Eliza confessed.

"Of course. Dr. King?"

"A glass of water would be great."

"I'll show you to the kitchenette. That way, you'll know where it is."

He led them past a series of storage closets to a

kitchen area. It was worn and utilitarian but brightly lit and clean.

Eliza fixed her coffee to her liking, which Bodhi noted hadn't changed since medical school—two sugars and a splash of milk. Guillaume steeped tea. And Bodhi sipped a glass of water and thought through how he and Eliza could possibly assist the authorities. The Tatiana Viant matter was so unusual, so out of the ordinary, that there was no clear path or process to follow to investigate her cause of death—or non-death.

"It's not entirely clear to me what role your department needs us to play, Guillaume," he said.

The doctor responded with a short laugh. "It's not clear to us either, I'm afraid. At first, I thought the timing couldn't be worse. The symposium is an enormous undertaking. I've taken the entire week off work to handle the logistics of two hundred pathologists arriving to attend three days of panel discussions, lectures, and roundtable talks. But then I viewed the timing through a different lens and realized it couldn't have been better."

Bodhi tilted his head. Even he, who sought to find the good in every situation, could see that having a dead woman turn up, unable to explain how she was alive or where she'd been, would create a distraction for the conference organizer.

"Truly. I have at my disposal a panel of specialists

with experience in black swan medical events. And if returning from the dead isn't a black swan, what is?"

"So you'll be asking Jon and Claude to lend a hand, too?" Eliza asked.

"No. Not yet. I may ask them, and Dr. Bechtel, too, if we decide their talents are needed."

"But they're all practicing pathologists, certified by your national organizations and members of respected Canadian associations. We're more or a less a pair of tourists who stumbled across a woman in distress on the side of the road."

He conceded her point with a nod. "Yes, but that's good. Leaving aside your organic connection to the woman—after all, you did find her—the fact that you're not associated with a province medical examiner's office or a university pathology department or otherwise within the system is an asset."

"How so?" Bodhi rinsed his glass and placed it in the small dishwasher.

Guillaume set down his mug of tea, waved his hands, and made a resigned sighing sound. "This case will quickly become a morass, I'm afraid. For instance, who has primary investigatory authority? It's not a missing person case. It's not a death investigation. What, if any crime, has occurred here? Then you turn to the jurisdictional questions. Tatiana Viant collapsed in

Montreal. She was declared dead in Port Grey. You found her on Île d'Orléans. She's now receiving treatment in Quebec City. Who is in charge? Do you see? If Doctors Bechtel, Malvern, and Ripple were involved, each of their institutions would also try to assert its will in the matter. And then, without fail, the lawyers would get involved. It is, as you would say, too many cooks in the kitchen."

Bodhi and Eliza both nodded their understanding. It seemed the universal language was neither love nor music but bureaucratic jockeying for primacy.

He continued. "So it is much cleaner if you are the cooks, yes? The coroner can't officially ask two Americans to step in, but we have a relationship, you and I. And you might do a favor for a colleague ... unofficially."

"Say no more. We've both been around the block enough times to catch your drift," Eliza assured him.

"The issue that still remains is the minor detail that there's no corpse," Bodhi reminded them both.

Guillaume nodded. "Perhaps you would like to visit our non-corpse in the hospital and speak to her parents when they arrive?"

## CHAPTER FOURTEEN

---

Eliza and Bodhi drove in silence for most of the short trip from the police department to the hospital. The sky was gray, and a light, cold rain fell, painting everything with a dismal veneer that Bodhi found to be a good match for Eliza's mood.

As he guided the rental vehicle up the steep entrance to a parking garage, she turned to him and voiced a thought that he suspected had been looping through her mind ever since they'd left Guillaume. "There are only two options. Either the woman we're about to see is not Tatiana Viant *or* Tatiana Viant was never dead. I mean, right?" She gave a small, forced laugh.

Bodhi took the ticket that the parking gate machine spit out. Then he eyed Eliza carefully for several long seconds before he responded. He knew his answer would add to her distress, but he couldn't bring himself to lie to her.

"I don't know." He pulled into a compact parking spot and killed the car's engine.

"What do you mean, you don't know? Of course you know. It doesn't take a medical degree to understand that those are the only two possible explanations."

"You believe that's true because it gives you the illusion that the universe is an orderly place with static rules. But it's not."

She fell into step beside him and they headed toward the elevator. "How can you say that? As a trained doctor, you know you have to acknowledge certain immutable rules. Scientific principles, causes and effects."

"Immutable? Without exception?"

She started to argue then cut herself off and tried a different tack. "Yes, okay, there are always exceptions. But that doesn't mean there are no rules."

"Not-knowing doesn't mean ignoring the evidence around us. It simply means we accept there are no shoulds. We aren't limited by unquestioned beliefs. As a medical examiner, you already know this, though. Parents outlive their children. Workers fall into industrial machinery and are mangled to death. Healthy young women drink an herbal energy beverage and collapse. People who believe they've been cursed die of fright. In a universe with rules, none of these things would happen, but they do happen. Daily. And you accept that. Is it really impossible to accept that Tatiana Viant's brain ceased functioning, her heart stopped beating, and her respiratory system shut down but she's alive now? Because if this woman *is* Tatiana, then that *did* happen. We didn't know that it could, but it has."

"Sure, brain function can return. Patients are revived every day. There's a reason protocol calls for the medical team to rule out confounding factors before making a neurological determination of death. I get all that. But once heartsick parents make the decision to remove mechanical ventilation and a comatose young woman codes, she's dead, Bodhi. And once her body's handed over to a mortician and is embalmed, she's really dead. Or does your not-knowing belief encompass the possibility of zombies roaming the earth?" She blew out a frustrated breath.

He took note of the color rising in her cheeks, her rapid, jerky breathing, and the faint tremor in her voice and decided not to answer the question directly. "Let's see what the Viants have to say."

Mr. and Mrs. Viant had not yet arrived from Port Grey when a cheerfully efficient nurse showed Bodhi and Eliza to Tatiana's private room.

"You have visitors," Nurse Grace trilled as she ushered them into the room and drew open the blinds.

Given the damp, dark day, the weak light that filtered through the window did not have its desired effect of flooding the room with sunlight, but it none-theless caught her patient's attention. Tatiana struggled to raise herself on her elbows and turned her unblinking eyes toward the window.

Nurse Grace smiled her encouragement. "Isn't that nice, Tatiana? A cleansing rain washing the city clean?"

Bodhi had to smile himself at the nurse's choice of lens. All situations were utterly changeable depending on what one chose to see.

After a long moment, Tatiana shifted her attention from the rain-splattered window to Bodhi and Eliza. Her blank expression showed no hint of recognition. The nurse let herself out of the room and quietly shut the door behind her.

"Tatiana?" Eliza said her name in a gentle voice.

Her eyes flickered.

"Do you remember us? I'm Eliza. This is Bodhi. We found you by the roadside last night and brought you to town."

Tatiana examined Bodhi's face. Then she turned back to Eliza.

"Tatiana," she croaked in a voice that was hoarse from disuse.

"Hi, Tatiana," Bodhi said.

Eliza glanced at him. He suspected she was feeling the same inadequacy he was. This woman couldn't tell them what had happened to her, and they lacked the tools to find out. They were both experienced in coaxing stories from the dead, but their familiar methods of examination and analysis were severely hampered by the fact that Tatiana was alive.

*Change the lens.*

He stepped closer to the bed. "May I see your hands?"

She watched his face as he spoke but didn't give any indication that she understood the request. He glanced at Eliza, unsure if he should proceed without Tatiana's explicit permission. Eliza stretched out her own hands, palms up, toward the bed.

Tatiana leaned forward and looked down at Eliza's hands. Then she mirrored the movement, reaching out with both hands, palms up. Bodhi took her right hand in his. Her skin was dry and papery. She had no callouses or blisters. He turned her hand over. Her fingernails were neatly trimmed and clean, but it was impossible to tell if that was the result of Nurse Grace's ministrations.

He returned her right hand to her lap and took her

left. He saw no difference. When he released her left hand, she began to move it absently. Pinching together her thumb and forefinger, then moving her hand to the left. With each motion, she mouthed a number. *'One, two, three, four* ....' When she reached twenty, she stopped.

Bodhi met Eliza's eyes. Eliza shook her head, as unsure as he was as to what Tatiana might be doing.

After a beat, Tatiana repeated the movements and her silent twenty-count.

When she finished, Eliza asked, "What are you counting, Tatiana?"

Tatiana cocked her head to the side and frowned at Eliza, concentrating intently. Then she said, "Pills."

*Pills?*

While Bodhi mulled over this answer, Eliza took Tatiana's chin in her hands and gently turned her face from side to side.

"Will you open your mouth for me?"

Tatiana did as she asked. Eliza examined the inside of the woman's mouth.

"Thank you." She looked at Bodhi. "No visible tooth decay, no gum inflammation. Wherever she's been, I think she's been brushing her teeth."

Bodhi mimed toothbrushing. "Tatiana, do you brush your teeth?"

After a delay, she slowly shook her head. "He does."

Bodhi's heart thumped behind his breastbone. Before he could ask about the *he* in her answer, a soft knock sounded on the door, and it swung open.

A man and a woman stood in the doorway, just behind Nurse Grace. The couple could only be the Viants, judging by their twin expressions of desperate hope and anxiety. The woman wrung her hands together. The man spotted Tatiana in the bed, and his jaw hinged open.

"What a busy day, dear. You have more visitors," the nurse chirped with a wide smile.

"Tatty?" the man rasped, frozen in the doorway.

His wife rushed past Bodhi and Eliza to the bedside and stared wordlessly at Tatiana with tears streaming down her cheeks.

Tatiana regarded the woman gravely. Then her gaze shifted to the man.

The air in the room grew still with anticipation. Time turned to thick syrup. Nurse Grace had one hand at her throat, waiting.

Tatiana's expression was blank. She looked from one to the other again, and still she did not speak.

She was silent for so long that Mrs. Viant's shoulders fell, her face crumbled, and she let out a soft moan of disappointment. Eliza took her by the elbow and guided her into a nearby chair. The woman covered her face in her hands and sobbed.

Her husband crossed the room and dropped a hand on her shoulder. "Shh, shh, now, lovebug," he comforted her.

Tatiana watched this exchange with naked interest. Then, to no one in particular, she announced. "Lovebug. Mom. Dad. Lovebug."

---

The rain had stopped. Eliza and Bodhi stretched their legs, taking a brisk walk through the damp neighborhood surrounding the hospital while the Viants reunited with their daughter in privacy. The hospital was located on the edge of Old Quebec's Upper Town, so they strolled toward the historic area.

They wandered through the wet, narrow streets, admiring the stone buildings, many of them fronted with colorful shutters and window boxes. They stopped to peek into a dim arched alleyway that hinted at long-ago military excursions or smuggling routes. Before they reached the steep stairs leading to Lower Town and the Quartier Petit-Champlain, with its art galleries, boutiques, and restaurants aimed at the tourist trade, they skirted the foot traffic and headed back toward the hospital.

Eliza broke the silence. "Tatiana was being held somewhere by someone who brushed her teeth."

"Maybe."

"Maybe?"

"We don't know the level of cognitive impairment she's suffered. The things she says may be real to her, but are they real?"

She shot him a dark look. "Is this a Zen koan? What *is* real?"

"Point taken," he chuckled. "But we do need to be cautious about attaching too much weight to her words right now. We need to better understand her current condition so we can be sure she's got her mental faculties."

"I agree with that." Eliza stopped to read a historical plaque affixed to the front of a building. Then she added, "When we get back to the hospital, why don't you talk to the Viants, and I'll have Nurse Grace walk me through the tests that have been ordered and what the medical team knows about Tatiana's condition?"

"Okay. I'm interested in talking to the Viants about how Tatiana came to be declared dead and the process that took place at the funeral home. Shouldn't someone have noticed she was alive when they were preparing the body for burial?"

"One would hope."

The list of unanswered questions stretched far beyond who might have brushed her teeth during the eight months she was believed to be dead. But he couldn't shake the thought that if they could answer that one question, the pieces of the puzzle would fall into place.

## CHAPTER FIFTEEN

Virgil ignored his mounting despair over Tatiana's disappearance and focused on packing the chemicals and equipment properly. Given the expense and importance of both items, he didn't dare trust the workers to pack them.

*The workers.* Moving several hundred thousand dollars' worth of merchandise and manufacturing supplies was far less of a worry than moving the workers. But it couldn't be avoided. Assuming Tatiana hadn't wandered off somewhere and died, she would be found. And although he seriously doubted she had the capacity to lead someone to the house, he had no interest in testing his belief.

The only option was to abandon the property in Sainte-Anne and set up at a new location where a building full of the walking dead wouldn't draw attention. He lifted his head and watched as a worker shuffled past.

Virgil did not care for the word 'zombie.' Although it accurately described his workers' situation, it brought to mind gruesome brain eaters from a campy horror film. He preferred to think of the workers as automatons or industrious insects, not unlike bees or ants. But even those analogies weren't fully correct.

He took care of them beyond what was required to keep the drug production clicking along. In addition to feeding them, he tended to their hygiene. He helped them wash their hands, feet, and faces every night before he brushed their teeth. He'd even combed Tatiana's long, dark hair for her when it became hopelessly tangled. Once their states became regulated, he gave them maintenance doses of Solo. Enough to keep them docile, obedient, and productive, but not so much that they couldn't also attend to their toileting needs and feed, bathe, and dress themselves—once he'd retaught them those skills.

He'd even been experimenting with lowering the dosage to see if there was a way to strike a balance between their reliance on him and their ability to form some autonomous thought. He could imagine a time when some of them might function as low-level managers of his enterprise, carrying out basic instructions and perhaps even answering questions that arose on the assembly line.

*Had he gone too far? Could Tatiana have affirmatively decided to leave? What would happen if his walking dead began making their own decisions?*

He pushed the thought away, unwilling to imagine the horrors that might come to fruition in that scenario. Just then, the college student shuffled by. Virgil realized with a pang that he didn't know the man's name. He'd have to ask Christian if he'd looked at the guy's identification before tossing it into the river. In the meantime, he decided, he'd settle on Bud. He had to call the guy *something*. It was important to Virgil that he keep in the forefront of his mind the fact that his workers, while no longer fully human, had once been people.

"Hey, Bud," he said.

The man kept walking, his eyes glued to the floor. Virgil reached out and touched his arm.

"Bud."

The guy slowly lifted his eyes to Virgil's face.

"That's you. Bud." Virgil pointed toward the man's chest.

The college student frowned then shook his head. "No," he rasped. He jabbed his thumb toward himself. "Mike." He paused then nodded at his own words.

"Mike?"

"Mike," he repeated.

Virgil watched Mike shamble away. The college student remembered his own name. And he was the first of Virgil's workers to retain verbal ability.

As the sound of Mike's halting, gravelly voice echoed in his ears, Virgil's heavy dread over Tatiana's disappearance and his compromised drug warehouse was replaced by a bracing splash of adrenaline and excitement. This development could lead to exciting possibilities for expansion of his Solo operation and for better understanding the minds of the handful of people he'd managed to revive.

He returned to the task at hand, swathing jars and bottles in thick layers of bubble wrap. His hands moved automatically, but his mind was elsewhere—working through a series of tests to determine Mike's level of cognition.

# CHAPTER SIXTEEN

When they returned to the hospital, Eliza and Bodhi split up to gather as much information as they could about Tatiana Viant.

Eliza found Nurse Grace typing notes into a computer. She stood by the nurses' station and waited quietly until the woman had finished her work.

"Oh, Dr. Rollins, can I help you?" she asked, looking up in mild surprise.

Eliza wondered briefly who'd told the nurse she was a doctor but didn't dwell on it. After all, she was about to ask Nurse Grace to share Tatiana's private health information. Having an air of authority could only aid in her goal.

"How's our patient doing?" Eliza asked, tilting her head toward the door to Tatiana's room.

"She's resting. Her parents are in the media room talking to a pair of police officers who turned up right after you and Dr. King left. I held them off as long as I could, but they desperately wanted to interview Tatiana. That mother of hers is a real spitfire, though. She herded those officers out of her daughter's room like she had a cattle prod." Nurse Grace laughed approvingly.

"I'm sure her maternal instincts are on overdrive at this point. Could you imagine how she must feel, finding her daughter alive after all these months?"

"My word, yes. Do you have children?"

"I've not been blessed." Eliza gave the nurse her stock answer to a question that had long bedeviled her.

"Oh. I'm sorry," the nurse murmured. After a respectful pause, she continued, "Well, mine are teenagers. My oldest is seventeen, not that much younger than Tatiana Viant. I have to say, I'd be doing everything in my power to protect her if she were in this wild situation."

"Speaking of Tatiana's situation," Eliza segued, leaning across the shelf that separated the work station from the public space, "what tests has the team ordered to assess her mental and physical condition? She appears to be stable, but what do the test results reveal?"

Nurse Grace exhaled a slow, leaky breath of air. "I

imagine procedures are quite a bit different back in the States. But the admitting physicians didn't order any tests at intake."

Eliza was sure she'd misheard. "I beg your pardon?"

The nurse smiled. "As you said, she's stable. Her vitals are good. She's eating. The current care plan is to monitor her and keep her comfortable. We have no idea what that poor girl's been through, but it's safe to say it was a nightmare. She may just need some time to recover. Quiet, rest, and food are the priorities. Later in the week, the psychiatric team will stop by to see her."

Before responding, Eliza reminded herself that she was a visitor here, with no actual authority, and that she was a coroner, with limited experience treating breathing patients. Keeping those two facts firmly in mind, she managed to speak in an even tone of voice rather than screaming.

"While Tatiana Viant's comfort and safety are of the foremost importance, surely the physicians here can order some basic blood work to make sure she hasn't been exposed to any contagious illnesses or other pathogens. What about the safety of the rest of your patients?"

A shadow of doubt crossed the nurse's face. "I'll mention it when the doctors round."

Eliza smiled. "You may also want to mention that there's an active investigation into her disappearance and reappearance. Surely the team here would prefer to get out in front of the issues that might be relevant and control which tests this young woman is subjected to, rather than leaving it to law enforcement to decide. Their priorities will be on administering justice, not helping Tatiana to heal. I mean, unless policing is very different here than it is in the States?"

Nurse Grace frowned. "No, you make a good point. I'll ... I'll share it with the team. If you're here when they round, perhaps you could talk with them?"

"I'd be glad to."

"Just in case you aren't, can you tell me what testing you'd recommend?"

"Of course. I'll write it down. Do you have a pen?"

The nurse handed a blank pad and a pen across the counter. Eliza scrawled the abbreviations for the most comprehensive battery of tests she thought the nurse would be able to sell to the medical team then signed her name with a flourish.

"Thank you." Nurse Grace took the sheet Eliza tore from the pad and studied it.

"My pleasure. I'd like to visit with Tatiana while her parents are being interviewed by the police. She might welcome the company."

The nurse regained her footing and managed a warning *tsk* sound before Eliza walked away. "Be sure you don't upset her," she urged.

Eliza opened the door to Tatiana's room and stepped into the silent room. The young woman was sleeping on her left side with her cheek resting on her hands. Her face was relaxed. Her breathing even.

Eliza lowered herself into the fake leather chair beside the bed and leaned forward. She watched Tatiana's chest rise and lower with each breath and tried to imagine the path that had led the woman from a casket in Ottawa to the side of the road in the Quebec countryside.

B odhi had positioned his chair slightly behind and to the right of the Viants. He sat and listened. The two police officers, who hadn't bothered to introduce themselves to him or otherwise acknowledge his presence when he'd entered the room, were peppering the couple with questions.

It didn't seem to Bodhi that they were actually processing the answers the Viants gave. They just marched their way down their endless list of questions. He somehow doubted this uninspired routine was what

Inspector Commaire had intended.

Mrs. Viant shifted in her chair and glanced at her husband.

Mr. Viant cleared his throat then interrupted the younger of the two policemen mid-sentence. "Pardon me, but we're done for now. My wife and I would like to spend some time with our daughter. I'm sure you understand." Although his words were conciliatory, there was no hint of negotiation in his tone.

The older of the two police officers, a tall, broadshouldered man with cropped salt-and-pepper hair and a military bearing, nodded gravely. "We do. And, as we've explained, we're quite interested in speaking to Ms. Viant ourselves."

"No." Mrs. Viant said the word in a firm yet quiet voice.

"No?" the senior officer repeated.

"Not yet," she amended. "Our Tatiana's been through an ordeal. Please, give her a few more hours to rest. She's really not even speaking yet. A handful of words have come back to her, but she's not communicative. Not really."

The younger officer twisted his mouth into a pucker of disbelief.

"It's true," Bodhi volunteered. "Tatiana Viant appears to be slowly regaining her verbal ability, but she's not in any condition to talk to you right now."

Mr. Viant twisted in his seat to give Bodhi a grateful smile.

"And how exactly are you qualified to make this judgment, Mister ...?" the senior officer trailed off.

"It's Doctor, actually. Dr. Bodhi King. Inspector Commaire asked me to consult on this matter in conjunction with Dr. Guillaume Loomis. Surely you were informed?"

Bodhi watched as the men processed the series of names he'd dropped and reached the conclusion that their interview was over.

"We'll leave you to visit with your daughter for now," the older one said in a gracious voice. He stood and doffed his hat to the Viants.

His younger partner handed Mr. Viant a business card. "We'll be in touch to arrange for a formal interview with your daughter. In the meantime, don't hesitate if you think of something that will be useful to our investigation. I assume you want to establish what happened to Tatiana just as much as we do."

"Quite a bit more, I assure you," Mrs. Viant said dryly.

The police officer had the grace to look chagrined at his own inartful phrasing.

"Of course, ma'am. I meant no offense."

"I'm sure you didn't."

The officers edged toward the door. "Dr. King, a word before we go?"

"Certainly. If you'll excuse me," he said to the Viants.

He followed the pair out into the hall.

The older of the two spoke first. "Our apologies for not involving you in the interview from the beginning. Inspector Commaire did say you might be helpful, but that nurse said you and the lady doctor had left the building. We didn't know whether you'd be back."

"Do you guys have names?" Their jackets were covering their badges.

"Right. Sorry. I'm McLord. This is Dixon." He jerked his head toward his partner.

"Great. Officer McLord, I'm not upset that you and Officer Dixon forged ahead without me and Dr. Rollins," Bodhi assured him, placing strong emphasis on Eliza's title and name to avoid a repeat of 'lady doctor.'

"Glad to hear you understand," Dixon chimed in.

"I do hope you'll respect the family's wishes about letting Tatiana recover a bit more before you press her for details. She's not in any condition to give you anything useful at this point."

Dixon nodded.

McLord said, "But you can."

Bodhi blinked. He'd expected he'd be asking the questions, not answering them. "I'm not so sure I can. Dr. Rollins and I haven't come up with a hypothesis as to how Tatiana Viant came to be here," he cautioned.

"But you found her, right? Driving back to Quebec City from a dinner date?" Dixon asked.

"We had a dinner, yes. It wasn't a date. We're old friends—medical school classmates."

"Okay, doc. Sure, whatever you say. We're interested in the girl, not your love life." Dixon snorted.

Bodhi held his eyes for several seconds, and then said slowly, "I'll be able to tell you whatever you like about how we found Tatiana. But it's important to me that we're clear about my relationship with Dr. Rollins. She's involved with a Police Chief of her hometown back in Louisiana. I wouldn't want some cross-border boys in blue grapevine to get the wrong impression."

"Dr. King, we're law enforcement officers, not middle school students. We don't have time to gossip."

It was Bodhi's turn to laugh. "Officer Dixon, I worked for years in close cooperation with the police. I know exactly how much gossip flies around a squad room."

Officer McLord chuckled and covered it with a cough. "In any case, maybe you and Dr. Rollins can go for a drive with us when we're finished here. Out to the spot where you found the Viant woman?"

"I can't speak for Dr. Rollins but I'd be happy to show you where we found her."

"Thanks."

"I'm curious about the funeral home in Port Grey. How did they not realize she was alive when they were preparing her body for burial?"

McLord nodded. "We had the same question. Dixon here interviewed the mortician over the phone this morning." He nodded to his partner.

Officer Dixon flipped his small notebook open and paged through it until he found the sheet of notes he was looking for.

He began to read from them. "Charles Francis, the funeral director, wasn't there. Out of town on a fishing expedition, I was told. But I spoke to his son and assistant, Ken Francis. According to Mr. Francis, the Viants did not want an open casket at the viewing, so they assigned her corpse to a junior person, a mortuary science student doing an internship. The kid ended up failing out of school. So in addition to being inexperienced, he apparently wasn't very good at what he was supposed to do."

"So, they're pleading incompetence?" Bodhi asked.

"That's their defense," McLord confirmed.

His partner went on. "The Port Grey authorities wanted to have an autopsy done but they don't have a dedicated full-time coroner."

Bodhi nodded. That was a common enough reality of small towns throughout the United States; he wasn't surprised to hear it held true to the north as well.

"They contacted the provincial authorities and were told the backlog was several weeks." Dixon paused here and looked up from his notes. "It seems Port Grey's one of those places where everybody knows everybody else. And the Chief of Police is on a bowling team with Mr. Viant. He decided it would be cruel to make the Viants wait to bury their daughter, so he signed off on closing the investigation without an autopsy."

"Does he have that authority?" Bodhi asked.

McLord shrugged. "He did it."

"Does Francis blame the coffin full of sand on his erstwhile intern, too?"

The police officers exchanged glances.

"Well?" Bodhi prompted.

"See, here's the thing. The body was stolen. He does blame that on the intern—apparently, the kid had a habit of leaving the delivery dock door open while he sneaked a cigarette. Someone must've slipped in and swiped the body while he was outside smoking," McLord explained.

"Or Tatiana came to and walked out of there," Dixon offered.

"Whatever happened, the intern panicked and called Francis. The son, not the father. Young Ken didn't want daddy to find out, so he came up with the sandbag plan."

Bodhi tried to believe his ears and failed. "You're not serious."

"Oh, I'm serious. You should have heard the way he blubbered about it on the phone," Dixon told him. "He asked us not to tell the Viants until he comes clean to his father. I agreed to delay, but eventually those people up in Port Grey are going to have to get their act together."

"Any idea why the service was closed casket? Her body wasn't mangled."

Dixon made a face that suggested he found the question distasteful, but he answered it. "Her mother insisted that Tatiana be remembered as vibrant and full of life. Seeing a waxy statue—her words—would blot out her memories of the living Tatiana."

Bodhi raised his shoulders. It made as much sense as the alternative. "Okay."

"So, that is where we are. We need to find out if

Tatiana left Port Grey under her own power or if someone abducted her and took her to Île d'Orléans—and if so, who and why," McLord said.

*He brushed my teeth.* Bodhi remembered Tatiana's words. "You two wait here for a few minutes. I need to find Dr. Rollins."

# CHAPTER SEVENTEEN

Eliza bumped into Bodhi as she was leaving Tatiana's room. She pulled the door shut slowly and silently behind her.

"I was just coming to find you," he said in a soft voice. "Is she sleeping?"

"Yes, she's out cold. What did you find out from the police?"

"Not much. Other than the fact that Port Grey is apparently amateur hour. Did you get any information from the medical team?"

She threw him a dark look. "It's not the big leagues here either, evidently. You won't believe this, but they haven't performed any cognitive assessments. They haven't even tested her blood."

"Nothing?"

"Nothing. I gave Nurse Grace a list of tests I recommended they order and hinted they should do something proactive so the cops don't take charge. That's all I could really do."

They looked at one another for a long moment, stymied and stuck, but not yet defeated. Eliza remembered that Bodhi shared her indefatigable nature.

"Okay." He accepted the news with complete calm.

She went on. "I just spoke with her parents. They think she was involved in a romance."

"Oh?"

She nodded. "The mother said Tatiana was painfully shy and introverted. Mom and Dad were nervous about her going so far away to such a big school for college. And for most of her freshman year, it looked as if their concerns were well-founded."

"Homesick?" he guessed.

"Homesick to the nth degree. And not just homesick. Mom said she was depressed, lethargic, and weepy when she came home for the winter break that first year. But then in the spring, things changed."

"They think she got herself a boyfriend—or girlfriend?"

"Yeah. Could be either. But *he* brushed her teeth, so my money's on a dude," Eliza mused.

"She never talked about a partner?"

"No. And she never brought one home. But both

parents said her entire demeanor flipped from sad and sullen to confident, cheery, and outgoing."

"That does sound like love," he agreed.

"That's what I thought, too. But they have no idea who the mystery person was."

"Nobody came to Port Grey for the funeral?"

"Oh, a whole group of college kids made the trip. They all came up together, but aside from Tatiana's roommate, the parents had never met any of them before."

Light sparked in Bodhi's eyes. "Maybe that social worker who recognized her would know. You know, the guy who worked at McAllen's counseling center."

She beamed. "That's a great lead. We should call Guillaume and ask him to put us in touch with the social worker. And then we ought to stop by the school to see if any of her friends can tell us anything about her personal life."

"It's not a plan, but we've got the seed of a plan. I like it. But I have to do something else first."

"What's that?" she frowned.

"The police officers want us to show them where we found Tatiana. I told them I'd take them. Do you want to join us?"

She hesitated. She'd been hoping they could make the trip to the university in Montreal and be back to the hotel by dinner time. She had big plans to order in room service, put on her pajamas, pour herself a glass of wine, and curl up for a leisurely phone call with Fred.

But she didn't want to miss out on any developments. Not knowing what Bodhi was learning with the police would be maddening—an unscratchable itch.

After a moment, she said, "I'll come along. Just let me make a quick call first."

"I'll tell Nurse Grace we're heading out and then let McLord and Dixon know you're joining us." He started down the hallway then turned and grinned at her over his shoulder. "Tell the Chief I said hi."

## CHAPTER EIGHTEEN

*Tuesday evening*

Jon packed up his briefcase, checked the outside pocket of the bag to confirm he had his chimerism materials for tomorrow's panel discussion, and clicked off his desk lamp. He was walking out the door when Lucy came racing down the corridor toward his office. Her white lab coat flapped behind her like tail feathers.

"I'm so glad I caught you," she breathed as she skidded to a stop.

"Why don't we pretend you didn't?" His tone was light, but he was only half-joking.

She pulled a face. "Come on, Malvern. You'll be sorry if you miss this." She waved a printout in the air.

"Are the results back on the glial cells?"

She nodded and arranged her face into an expression of satisfaction—a suppressed grin and an arched eyebrow communicated her excitement. "And I think we have something." Her grin wobbled. "At least I hope we have."

His eyes widened. He pushed his office door open and flicked on the overhead light.

"What've we got?" he asked as they walked inside.

She spread the results out on his desk, and they stood shoulder to shoulder studying the reports in silence. Jon could feel his brow furrowing and smoothed it.

"There's evidence of inflammation and neurodegeneration," he muttered.

"Consistent across all your cultures."

He shook his head. "I can't tell from the gene expressions what might be causing it."

She flashed a bright smile. "That's because you're the biologist. Let the toxicologist walk you through it. After the team in the lab confirmed that all the victims' glial cells had the same pattern of damage and deterioration, I started applying toxins. Because we know sodium channels have been implicated in neurodegenerative diseases, I started from the hypothesis that the drug that killed these folks may have contained a sodium channel blocker."

He may not have been a toxicologist, but he knew enough to ask the right questions. "Couldn't it also have been a calcium channel blocker or a potassium channel blocker?"

"It could have. And if these first toxins hadn't shown the results they did, I'd have moved on to those ion channels and then to the glutamate receptors. But we don't have to do any of that because these suckers exhibited time-dependent, delayed cell death." The triumph in her voice was unmistakable.

"Across all the culture populations?"

"Yes, sir. We have a winner!"

"What's the drug?"

Her giddiness was contagious. For a moment, he dared to hope they'd found the scourge that had been killing large swaths of the drug-using community.

Then her face dropped. "So here's the thing. It's not a street drug. It's not even a component of any street drug I've ever run across. I think it's a completely novel designer drug."

"Right, a synthetic."

They'd talked about this at length. Black market chemists loved creating new synthetic drugs. They usually stayed half a step ahead of Health Canada. Once the agency studied a new drug and declared it illegal—which could take months, if not years—the street chemists would slightly alter the substance's molecular structure. This resulted in an entirely new drug, which was legal until it came to Health Canada's attention, and the whole cycle repeated. From what he understood, the United States system suffered from the same loophole. It was maddening, but it was hardly a secret.

"No, Jon. We've all been wrong about that. It's not a synthetic. At least, I don't think so. I think it's a composite of three naturally occurring neurotoxins: TTX; STX; and CDX."

He searched his memory then shook his head. "Sorry, Luce. That's nothing but alphabet soup to me."

"That's fair. TTX is tetrodoxin, most commonly known as puffer fish or Japanese fugu fish poison. STX, or saxitoxin, is a paralytic shellfish poison, which operates in a very similar fashion as TTX. It's another voltage-gated sodium channel blocker."

"What about CDX?"

"That's a weird one. It's candotoxin, an atypical alpha-neurotoxin from the blue krait, a venomous elapid snake found in the tropics and subtropics."

"Wait. Hang on. Your theory is someone is combining two marine toxins and a snake venom and selling the concoction to people looking for a buzz?"

She shot him a sidelong glance. "Well, when you say it like that it sounds farfetched."

"Lucy, that's because it *is* farfetched. It's so far past farfetched as to be ... not possible."

"I'm telling you, Jon. That deadly trinity is the cocktail of chemicals that's killing these people. I'm certain of it."

She crossed her arms and challenged him to disagree.

"You're not just grasping at straws here, are you?" he said after studying her confident posture.

"Come down to the lab. I'll show you."

Jon sighed and dropped his briefcase to the floor. Then he grabbed his lab coat from the hook on his door and followed Lucy out into the hallway.

# CHAPTER NINETEEN

Officers McLord and Dixon trailed the rental car out of the city and past Montmorency Falls. Bodhi drove slowly, both so the police cruiser could follow him easily and so that he wouldn't miss the spot where they had encountered Tatiana. The perspective would be different coming upon it from the opposite direction.

In his concentration, he missed what Eliza was saying.

"I'm sorry. Could you say that again?"

She shifted in the passenger seat. "I was just thinking that it seems like a lifetime ago when we crossed that bridge across the falls with the spray in our faces and no living dead to worry about."

He nodded his agreement. So much had happened since their driving tour of the island. The puzzles and stress were crowding out the memories of exploring the small towns with Eliza and repairing the rift between them.

"Did you get ahold of your boyfriend?" he asked.

She narrowed her eyes as if she might object to the personal question, but after a moment, she simply answered it. "I did."

They lapsed back into silence, and he returned his attention to scanning the roadside as the car crept along the ribbon of road.

"You don't date?" she asked after several moments.

"I haven't." It wasn't so much that he had a blanket ban on dating. He just hadn't made finding romantic companionship a priority. Reconciling a relationship with the precepts he followed would require care.

"And you're not lonely? Because I didn't date for several years. And I was lonely." Her chin jutted out as if she dared him to judge her.

He didn't. Instead he examined her question.

Was he lonely? Loneliness seemed to imply something or someone was lacking in his life. Was there an absence?

"Bodhi?" she promoted.

"I'm thinking. I don't know if I'm lonely. I'm alone. But I'm not sure those are the same."

She made a small noise in the back of her throat.

Before she could say whatever words she was forming, he turned on his flashers and brought the car to a stop at the side of the road.

"It's over there, isn't it?" He pointed across the narrow lane to a clearing just before the bend in the road. Behind the spot where they'd seen Tatiana, a copse of dense trees stretched back as far as he could see.

Eliza followed the line of his finger and looked hard at the spot. "Yeah, that's it."

They crossed the road and waited for McLord and Dixon to join them.

"This is where we found her," Bodhi announced as the two officers approached. "Eliza saw her."

"What caught your attention, Dr. Rollins?" McLord asked. Dixon took out his notebook and waited, pen poised over a clean page, for Eliza's answer.

"It was dusk, about this time. The light was fading. I saw a flash of white as we rounded that bend coming from the restaurant. At first, I thought it might be a deer. Are there deer on this island?"

"It's not all moose and grizzlies, you know."

She ignored the crack. "As the headlights arced over the spot, I realized it was a woman in a white dress. The lights caught her face and I could clearly see she was in distress."

"So, you pulled over where exactly?" Dixon addressed the question to Bodhi.

Bodhi scanned the berm and walked back roughly two car lengths. "Here."

The others joined him. They stood on the approximate spot and surveyed the landscape.

"Where the devil did she come from?" McLord muttered.

To the left was nothing but woods. To the right, in the distance, cleared farmland.

"Wouldn't she had to have come from that farming village?" Eliza asked, pointing to the cluster of barns, farmhouses, and silos that dotted the hills.

"You'd think so, but no. That clutch of farms is all owned by one family. We had a team out yesterday, crawling all over their places. Nobody had ever seen Tatiana Viant before. They opened up every stall, every shed, and every basement and attic crawl space for our people to search. They found no evidence that anyone had been hiding on any of the farms."

"How far is it to the next village to the left of the woods?" Bodhi asked.

"Far," Dixon answered. "At least forty kilometers. Too far for a stunned, barefoot woman to walk without being spotted. It's a thriving little town. Someone would have noticed her."

The four of them stood in the dim light and stared at the trees.

"What's behind the woods?" Bodhi persisted.

McLord spoke first. "There's nothing behind those woods."

"There used to be," Dixon corrected him.

Bodhi turned his head in the younger officer's direction. "What used to be there?"

"The village of Sainte-Anne. My grandmother used to tell us stories about it. It's a creepy old abandoned railroad village."

"The entire town is abandoned?" Eliza asked.

McLord picked up the strand. "Yeah, you'd be surprised how many of these ghost towns there are in Canada. Company towns where the main employer went out of business and the residents slowly abandoned the place. Or towns where a fire or mudslide destroyed the commercial center and people grew tired of traveling thirty miles to mail a letter and buy a jug of milk. The residents just move out and the towns are left to crumble."

"So Sainte-Anne is an abandoned village?" Bodhi asked to be sure he understood.

"Yes. As far as I know, it hasn't been officially condemned yet, but the homes are rotting and falling down. Maybe some teenagers will wander into an old mansion on a dare, but it's effectively a ghost town."

A blue van rounded the bend, slowing when the driver spotted the police car and the four figures by the roadside. McLord raised a hand in greeting. The driver waved and continued on his way.

Eliza broke the silence as the van's taillights shrank into nothingness. "A ghost town? What better place to keep a woman who's supposed to be dead?"

McLord nodded. "We'll go in and check it out before it gets any darker. You two can wait here or ride with us. The roads are deteriorating. Leave the rental so you don't break an axle."

Bodhi glanced at Eliza. She nodded.

"We'll come along," he said.

They crossed back to the cars and Bodhi locked the doors to the rental before joining Eliza in the back seat of the squad car.

## CHAPTER TWENTY

Virgil wiped his damp palms on the thighs of his pants then gripped the steering wheel again. Over the thrum of his heart, he told himself to check the rearview mirror to ensure the police car hadn't pulled out and followed him.

He flicked his eyes to the mirror then exhaled with relief. No police car. The road behind him stretched out empty and desolate in the gathering darkness.

As his pulse slowed, his eyes returned to the mirror, this time to check the cargo, both human and otherwise, in the back of the van.

Three workers sat, their legs outstretched and their backs against the side of the panel van. They slumped against one another as the van bounced and rocked down the road. Across from them, Mike sat, nearly upright, keeping a tight grip on the stainless steel case that Virgil had placed beside him back at the house.

"Don't let this fall over," he'd told Mike, taking care to enunciate every word, as he'd loaded the case into the van next to him.

While it was true Virgil would prefer that the case remain upright, he had packed the toxins and venom with extraordinary care. Even if the case toppled over, there would be no spills.

But the task would prove a good test for Mike. Could the young man follow simple instructions? If so, Virgil would continue to increase his responsibilities and decrease his maintenance dose until he reached a balance that would allow him to function almost normally.

Virgil returned his eyes to the road ahead and resumed his worrying about the authorities. There had definitely been two uniformed officers standing at the roadside, along with two other people. He wasn't naive enough to think their appearance there was unrelated to his operation. In the eight months he'd done business out of the house in Sainte-Anne, he'd encountered the police on the stretch of road between the old village and Quebec City exactly zero times before now.

They had to be there because of him. Because of Tatiana.

No matter, he assured himself. They'd never go poking around the dilapidated village. And even if they did, they'd find nothing in the house that would lead them to him. He'd cleaned it thoroughly, removing every trace of his presence.

*What about the grounds?* his mind whispered at him, snakelike and insidious.

It doesn't matter. They wouldn't find anything. And if they did, there would be no way to tie it back to him.

He repeated the sentence silently to himself until he believed it. Then he switched on the radio to drown out his thoughts with music.

One downside of surrounding himself with the undead was that there was precious little in the way of scintillating conversation in his day-to-day life.

# CHAPTER TWENTY-ONE

O fficer McLord had, if anything, understated the condition of the roads in Sainte-Anne, Bodhi thought. He braced himself with one hand against the roof of the car as he jostled from side to side. Eliza flew sideways, and her elbow connected with his rib.

"Sorry!"

"Not your fault," he gasped as his teeth clattered against one another.

"Not long now. We're about to enter the town square," McLord assured them from the front seat.

The minutes stretched out in an endless pattern of bumps and jerks until Dixon finally brought the vehicle to a stop smack in the middle of a traffic circle.

"You're not going to leave the car here?" Eliza asked.

Dixon put the car in park and killed the engine. The car's nose was nearly touching the front of a toppled-over statue of some long-ago community leader.

"Why not?" Dixon retorted. "There's not going to be anyone else on the road. And this is a central location."

As they exited the car, Bodhi surveyed the square. In the quickly fading light, the boarded-up shops, broken windows, and cracked pavement created an atmosphere of decay and loss. He didn't imagine it was much different mid-day.

"Here," McLord said, after rummaging in the glove box. "We've only got one extra, so you two stick together." He handed Eliza a large, rugged flashlight.

"Aren't we coming with you?" she asked as she hefted the light.

"It's better if you don't," McLord answered. "Officer Dixon and I are going to do a door-to-door canvas. Given that the homes are abandoned, we'll be letting ourselves in to look around. The last thing we need is two foreign doctors to crash through a rotted attic floorboard and hurtle to their deaths."

He had a point, Bodhi conceded to himself. But they hadn't tagged along just to cool their heels near a headless statue all evening.

"What can we do to be helpful?" he asked.

"First, check that light and make sure it works," McLord said.

Eliza flipped the switch and aimed the bright light across the square at what had at one time been the courthouse. Long shadows sprang up against the cracked stone wall.

"It works," Dixon confirmed the obvious.

McLord gave him a sidelong look then said, "Why don't you canvas the commercial district? It's just a few short blocks. Do not go inside any structures, regardless of what you see inside or how sturdy you think a building might be. Are we clear?"

"Crystal," Bodhi confirmed.

Eliza nodded.

"Just visually inspect from the street. If you see something noteworthy, let us know when we get back." McLord checked the time. "We'll rendezvous in one hour."

Bodhi started the stopwatch function on his wristwatch.

"Be careful," Eliza called after them in a voice that was at a slightly higher, squeakier pitch than her normal speaking voice.

Bodhi watched as the police officers' flashlights bobbed along in the dark, twin beams of yellow. McLord and Dixon mounted the stairs to the remnants of a fine stone mansion set back on a corner lot. It was the sort of house the mayor or the owner of the most prosperous store might have once called home.

McLord lifted the heavy knocker and let it fall against the door. The thump echoed in the still air. After a few seconds, Dixon lifted his foot and aimed a powerful kick. The wood splintered loudly, Dixon shouldered the door open, and the pair disappeared inside.

They watched in silence for a moment.

Then Eliza asked, "Where should we start?" She shined the light in a wide arc from left to right.

Bodhi closed his eyes and focused on the quiet town's whisperings, hoping the universe would send him a hint.

When he opened them, Eliza was watching him. "Well?"

He shrugged. "No clue. I guess it doesn't matter where we start as long as we cover the entire square."

"Fair enough." She pointed the flashlight at the nearest building. "Let's go."

They covered the entire square in less than twenty minutes thanks to Eliza's detail-oriented nature.

She pointed out that the buildings all appeared to be blanketed with a thick coat of grime. Then she posited,

"If Tatiana had been kept in one of these storefronts or office buildings, at a minimum, there would be fingerprints in the dust and dirt that coated the doors. Do you agree?"

"I do."

So they fell into a pattern.

They walked from one building to the next. She directed the light at the door. He walked up and inspected the surface closely for signs of disturbance in the grime.

After examining a fruit and vegetable market, two law offices, a physician's office, the chemist's shop, the bookstore, an accounting firm, a butcher shop, a bakery, and all three entrances to the courthouse, they'd discovered only four spiders, a dried-up wasp's nest, and the skeleton of a small rodent (which he pegged as a mouse, but she insisted was a vole).

"There's not a single living thing here," he declared.

"It really would make a good place to stash someone, though," she mused.

"Maybe Dixon and McLord are having better luck."

Even as he said the words, he doubted they'd be borne out. But at least the police officers' flashlights were moving at a steady pace.

They'd made their way through the first row of

brownstones and a handful of grand mansions that fronted the square. Now their lights were bouncing off the windows of homes several blocks away. How much longer could it take before they finished their canvas?

Bodhi and Eliza returned to the spot near the statue. He checked his stopwatch. "We still have thirty-five minutes."

Eliza groaned softly. After a moment, she pointed the light away from the neighborhood to what appeared to be a park or garden up the hill behind the courthouse.

"We might as well walk up there to that green space and see if we find anything."

He shrugged. "It beats standing here."

They set off for the hill, taking slow, mincing steps on the dark, uneven path.

Not until they reached the wrought-iron front gates did Bodhi realize their destination was neither a garden nor a park. It was a cemetery.

Recognition must have hit Eliza at the same moment, because she giggled. "Okay, now it's officially creepy."

Social customs and a passing acquaintance with horror films dictated that he suggest turning back rather than traipsing through an abandoned town's graveyard in the dark.

But then again, they were a pair of pathologists—two doctors who dealt in death on a truly daily basis. The venue should strike them as no more hair-raising than their local dry cleaners or library.

"Are you still game?" he asked, just to confirm.

"Why the heck not?"

He pushed open the gate. It swung inward with a creak that would have been a cliché had it not been real.

"Ladies first," he said with a bow.

"Right. Now you're a gentleman," she snarked.

"Also, you have the flashlight."

"Fair point."

She passed through the gate and he followed close behind her. They wandered through the neat rows of headstones, stopping to check a date of birth or death from time to time, to comment on a moving, sad, or funny epitaph, or to admire a particularly grand mausoleum.

Here, in the home of the dead, the stillness was comfortable, not unnerving as it had been in the town square. This was a place that was meant to be dormant and lifeless.

"Looks like the town was abandoned by the nineteen forties. I haven't seen any headstones with a date later than 1939, have you?" he mused.

"No, I haven't. Sure looks like the Lavoire family did okay for themselves, huh?" She jabbed the light at an enormous marble angel perched atop a large tombstone, which was flanked by several equally large and ornate tombstones.

"I guess so. It seems as if nobody comes out here to mow the grass or leave flowers or wreaths, though—no signs that family visits these graves. Even though the town's been abandoned, it's strange that their dead have been forgotten."

"Maybe that's just an American thing," she said in a voice that suggested she didn't believe her own theory.

"Maybe." That didn't feel right. In his experience, cultures that buried their dead did so in an effort to continue to feel close to them. "Tell me about the turkey vulture men from your talk."

She blinked in surprise and jerked the flashlight. It cast an eerie light up at her face, as if she were a camp counselor telling a ghost story.

"Well, the water table in Southern Louisiana is very high. The ground can be spongy, swampy. Much like in New Orleans, if you bury the dead in it, they'll eventually rise up to the surface, waterlogged and putrid."

"That's graphic."

"It's a fact of life on the bayou. But unlike the Creoles, Africans, and Europeans who settled in New

Orleans, who solved this problem by creating above-ground cemeteries, the Atchafalaya tribe had designated turkey vulture men. When a tribe member died, the turkey vulture men buried the body. On the first anniversary of the death, they disinterred the body and plucked the remaining flesh off the bones. When the bones were picked clean, they were presented to the family in a special ceremony."

"Exactly."

"Exactly what?"

"Exactly my point. Nobody just buries their dead and forgets about them. They continue to honor them."

She waved away the point. "Maybe the town hasn't been condemned but the road leading up here is unpassable by car. Or maybe the families did make pilgrimages here for decades and decades, but eventually the connection to Sainte-Anne faded and ultimately broke. I mean, the youngest corpse in this place is nearly eighty. Most of them are much older."

"Maybe." He walked several paces away, toward the back of the cemetery, trying to pinpoint why the graveyard felt wrong to him.

He turned and stumbled over a loose clod of earth. He regained his footing then crouched near the spot where he'd tripped.

He reached down and filled his hand with fresh, soft

dirt. It poured between his fingers. He squinted at the dark ground in front of him, and his pulse sped up.

"Eliza," he called over his shoulder. "Bring the flashlight over here, please. This ground's been disturbed."

## CHAPTER TWENTY-TWO

Eliza hurried down the hill to the town, trying with limited success to keep the beam of light steady as she ran. The stillness that had been peaceful in the cemetery was frightening outside its gates, and her heart thudded in her chest.

*At least you've got the light,* she told herself.

Bodhi had insisted on staying in the graveyard while she ran to find McLord and Dixon. He was concerned they wouldn't be able to relocate the freshly turned ground if he left the spot. But that meant he was sitting in complete darkness until she returned.

The thought propelled her forward even faster. She tried not to speculate on what they'd find in the cemetery. Nothing good, she imagined.

She raced past the car and turned toward the row of

houses where she'd spotted the police officers' flashlights as she made her way back to town.

As the ground beneath her feet flattened, she began to jog. She dodged the roots growing up between cracks in the uneven pavement as she rushed forward.

She met up with the officers as they were coming out of a sprawling home, set away from the rest. It had a sort of faded gothic glamour to it even as shingles hung from the roof at odd angles and several floorboards were missing entirely from the large, wrap-around porch.

She came to a stop outside the front gate.

Officer Dixon frowned at her. "I thought we told you to stay in the square."

"We found something." She gasped between breaths.

"In the square?" Officer McLord asked in a knowing tone.

"No. In the cemetery at the top of the hill. We'll need shovels."

The police officers exchanged a look.

After a moment, McLord said, "Well, you're in luck." He jerked his head toward the junior officer, who set off for a ramshackle shed set back from the street to the right of the house. He was muttering unhappily under his breath.

While they waited, Eliza caught her breath and then asked, "Did you find anything interesting?"

"Not until we got here," McLord gestured to the house behind him.

"This place? What did you find here?"

"Well, handily, we found a toolshed with shovels, a wheelbarrow, and other garden implements. But inside, we found ... nothing. Too much nothing."

She pursed her lips. It would be just her luck if McLord was a Buddhist, too. "How much nothingness is too much?" she asked.

"Let's put it this way. There was no dirt. No dust. No cobwebs. No bugs."

"Oh. Someone cleaned it."

"More like someone scrubbed it down. Not only was there no dirt, it was sparkling clean. Cleaner than any inhabited house would be."

"Someone removed all traces of having been there?"

"Exactly. We're talking about a thorough job—a deliberate sterilization. This wasn't a group of kids who broke in to party and then cleaned up the evidence. We'll send in a team, but I guarantee you they won't find a single print. Not even a partial."

Eliza let that prediction roll around in her mind for a moment. Someone who went through that much trouble to cover his or her tracks would be a difficult person to find.

"Tatiana couldn't have been here alone. She doesn't have the capacity to think through a plan to remove all traces of her presence let alone the ability to execute it."

"So let's just assume for now, someone was holding her here. And maybe not just her. This a big house. And all the rooms were clean. If they were all in use, there could have been a crowd." McLord's voice was grim as he considered this possibility.

She shivered at the thought of more Tatianas.

"Did you check the bathroom sink?" she asked suddenly.

McLord eyed her. "Yeah. Why?"

"Was it wet—the drain?"

"As a matter of fact, it was."

"Tatiana said someone—she called him he—brushed her teeth."

McLord chewed on this piece of information.

She had another question. "How is there running water? Surely the utilities were turned off long ago."

"There's a well in the yard. And a generator in the basement, too. Somebody had set up most of the creature comforts."

Dixon returned, pushing a wheelbarrow full of

digging tools and wearing a scowl. "You said uphill, right?"

"Sorry, yes," Eliza told him with a sheepish smile.

He stuck his flashlight in the waistband of his pants and trudged forward with his load.

---

**B**odhi heard them coming before he saw their lights. The sudden noise was jarring against the complete silence that blanketed the cemetery. The rise and fall of voices, the dull thud of shoes pounding against the ground, and the rattle and clang of what he hoped were digging tools bumping together cut through the night.

He finished his meditation on death and opened his eyes. Then he stood and brushed loose dirt from the seat of his pants with his dirty hands. A losing battle.

The cones of light from their flashlights swam into view, and he turned in the direction of the light, blinking to adjust his eyes.

"Bodhi?" Eliza called as one beam of light swung wildly from side to side. She must have turned in a semicircle, looking for some sign of him.

"Over here!" He waved his arms overhead in a wide arc.

Light blasted him in the face for a half-second. He reared back his head, eyes watering. Whoever was holding the flashing quickly redirected it to the ground.

Eliza and the police officers crested the hill behind the Lavoire family's plot and came into view. McLord and Eliza in the lead; Dixon bringing up the rear with a wheelbarrow.

"What've we got?" McLord asked while he was still several yards away.

"I think at least four new graves. No markers." Bodhi pointed to a wide strip of raw earth.

McLord aimed his flashlight at the patch. Eliza did the same.

"Well ... hell."

Dixon dropped the handles of the wheelbarrow. "Pat, we can't dig up four bodies in the dark with the help of two civilians."

McLord nodded slowly. "We *can*. But we're not going to. Call it in. Tell them we need a team from the coroner's office, at least one truck with flood lights, and some sandwiches and coffee. Have them send a patrol car out to take Dr. Rollins and Dr. King back to the city. It's gonna be a long night."

Dixon nodded and reached for his phone.

"You'll let us know what you find?" Bodhi asked.

McLord hesitated. "It may not be related to the Viant woman."

"It's related," Eliza interjected.

They both turned toward her.

"How do you figure?" McLord asked.

"Too coincidental. We found a woman who was supposed to be buried outside Ottawa wandering along the road within walking distance of an abandoned town where there are fresh graves. And that house you said was too clean? Someone was using this as a base of ... some sort of operation. When Tatiana vanished, he panicked. Whoever he is, he's responsible for her and for these unmarked graves. I know it," Eliza said with conviction.

"Occam's Razor. The simplest explanation is usually right, Officer McLord," Bodhi added.

McLord spread his hands wide and shrugged. "Maybe when you deal with dead people. But living people are as unpredictable as all get out. You just never can tell."

"All the same—"

"All the same, I'll let Inspector Commaire know that you've asked to be updated," McLord agreed. "You've been rather helpful, after all."

Bodhi furrowed his brow. "When you're looking for this person—whoever had Tatiana and likely dug these graves, you might want to track down some of the families that used to live here. These abandoned towns that you said aren't uncommon ... who handles the upkeep of the cemeteries there? Mows the lawn, makes sure the headstones don't tumble over? Is that the government?"

McLord shook his head slowly. "No. Except for one or two that've been turned into tourist destinations, they're truly abandoned. If anyone hired a caretaker, it would have been former residents."

"Maybe something to look into," Bodhi reiterated.

# CHAPTER TWENTY-THREE

*Wednesday morning*

Bodhi scanned the room, looking over the heads of the chattering pathologists for Eliza. He spotted her in a corner, clutching a glass of juice and a bagel and nodding at whatever Felix Bechtel was telling her.

He picked up his mug of tea and waded into the sea of people to join them. Halfway across the room, he was waylaid by Guillaume.

"Ah, Bodhi, are you ready for the presentation?" The organizer gave him a hearty thump on the shoulder.

"I'm looking forward to it. Looking forward to the whole symposium, actually."

Guillaume beamed. Then his smile drooped. "I

heard from Inspector Commaire that you and Dr. Rollins discovered some bodies last night."

"Not quite. We found some fresh graves. The police brought us back to the city before they started excavating. Did Inspector Commaire share any details with you?"

Guillaume glanced around the room then inclined his head toward the hallway. "Shall we chat somewhere more private?"

"Of course." Bodhi gestured for him to lead the way.

They headed for the door, and Bodhi caught Eliza's eye. She nodded and put a hand on Felix's arm as Bodhi crossed the threshold and followed Guillaume outside.

A moment later, Eliza appeared. Her efforts to extricate herself from her conversation had apparently failed. Felix was right beside her.

"Sorry," she mouthed.

"Guillaume, Bodhi." Felix gave them each a brief smile and a nod. "I was just telling Eliza I have some information that may prove helpful in the Tatiana Viant matter."

"Oh?" Guillaume's eyebrows crawled up his forehead.

Eliza pulled apart a chunk of her bagel and nibbled it while Felix geared up to retell his story. Bodhi couldn't tell from her demeanor if she was disconcerted, bored, or, knowing Eliza, just hungry.

"Yes. After we spoke yesterday morning, I asked around about Ms. Viant. My department shares a hallway with the Department of Psychiatry. I mentioned her name to a colleague, just in passing."

Bodhi wondered how Tatiana Viant's name would come up in passing, unless Felix and his friend were in the habit of trading tidbits of juicy gossip from their respective departments. Judging by Eliza's faint smirk, she was wondering the same thing.

Guillaume, on the other hand, seemed unperturbed. "What did this colleague have to say?"

"Before the reorganization of the mental health services on campus, psychiatry used to run some work-shops and some studies through the counseling center. My colleague said Tatiana Viant participated in one."

"One of which—a workshop or a research study?" Bodhi asked.

"Er, well, evidently, some of the workshops were also research studies."

"With proper consent, I trust?" Guillaume asked.

"I don't know the details, of course. But I'm certain everything was aboveboard and that all the researchers complied with the code of ethics. However ..."

"Spit it out," Guillaume said.

Possibly because he was startled by the bluntness, Felix did just that. "However, the board of trustees thought the optics were bad. It gave the appearance that residents were experimenting on students under the guise of helping them. It was frowned upon. So several workshops were cancelled and some experiments were shut down."

"Including the one Tatiana Viant had been enrolled in?" Bodhi asked.

"Yes, according to my colleague."

"I don't suppose your colleague has any idea what it was about?"

"She doesn't. And she said the person who'd been running the program left the university."

"Under a cloud?" Guillaume asked.

"His fellowship wasn't renewed."

Felix's delivery was bloodless and dry, but his audience understood the subtext: the researcher had been unceremoniously shown the door.

"Do you have a name? Anything?" Bodhi pressed.

"I don't. Her department chair came out of the men's room and she stopped talking mid-sentence. I can certainly go back to her, if you have specific questions."

Bodhi and Eliza both looked at Guillaume. This was his show; they were just the unpaid help.

He winced and sucked in a deep breath. "I'm not

sure. Let me speak to Inspector Commaire after today's meeting breaks up and get back to you. Thank you, though, Felix for bringing this to our attention."

Felix smiled and bowed from his waist. "Happy to be of service. Now, if you'll excuse me, I think I'll just brush my teeth before the sessions begin. It wouldn't do to have poppy seeds between my teeth."

As he walked off, Eliza looked down at the sesame seed bagel in her hand then whispered to Bodhi, "Check my teeth."

He peered into her mouth. "Seed-free."

Guillaume managed a small laugh. "If you're quite finished, we have just enough time to fill you two in on last night's discovery before the opening session."

Eliza turned, wide-eyed and serious, and said, "Yes, please."

"Four bodies were recovered from the cemetery in Sainte-Anne. Their vintage was quite a bit younger than that of the official residents of the cemetery—preliminarily, the coroner says they've all died within the past six months."

"How badly decomposed are they?" she asked.

This time, Guillaume's smile was heartfelt. "The cool weather and the soil pH helped no doubt, but the bastard who buried them did us a favor."

"Plastic wrap?" Bodhi guessed. Despite the fondness

movie gangsters seemed to have for disposing of bodies in trash bags or wrapped in plastic, the material actually preserved bodies nicely. There was, after all, a reason people wrap their leftovers in plastic wrap, and it wasn't to hasten rotting.

"We weren't that lucky. He covered them with lime."

Another mob movie favorite. But, here, too, the reality was counter to the expectation. Lime had the unexpected effect of slowing degradation.

"Six months or fewer, covered with lime," Eliza murmured. "So, facial features should still be discernible."

"I'm told they're in quite good condition."

"Any idea as to who any of them might be?" Bodhi asked.

"Sadly, they're all quite young—late teens or early twenties. So, in light of Tatiana, Inspector Commaire is going to start with the universities in Montreal to see if there are any missing person reports that might match."

"Is he going there in person?" Eliza asked.

Guillaume shrugged. "I'm afraid I've no idea. May I ask why?"

"Bodhi and I were hoping to talk to some of Tatiana's university friends. And now, with this news and Felix's friend who says she was part of a psych experiment ... well, perhaps we could tag along?"

"I'd be happy to ask him," Guillaume mused.

Just then, a harried-looking redhead with thick glasses and a bright smile popped his head out into the corridor. "Oh, Dr. Loomis, there you are. The attendees are filtering into the main conference room and taking their seats. Looks like we'll be kicking off right on time!"

He tapped his watch then walked smartly down the hall, expecting Guillaume to follow.

"Ah, death—not to mention a group of forensic pathologists—waits for no man." He hurried away behind the redhead.

"Do you need one final tooth check or are you good?" Bodhi asked Eliza.

She tittered. "I'm good."

He grew more serious. "Are you?"

He didn't want to bring up the panic attacks that had plagued her during medical school if they were no longer a concern. But he wanted her to know he was in her corner if she needed him.

Her eyes softened and she nodded. "I am. I've gotten pretty good at getting a handle on my nerves before things spiral out of control—most of the time."

He squeezed her hand. "I'm glad."

"Me, too."

# CHAPTER TWENTY-FOUR

*Côte-des-Neiges, Montreal*

Virgil's hearty laugh boomed in the empty apartment. Too loud, he thought, too late.

The leasing agent flashed him a nervous smile. "So, Mr. uh, Mann, what do you think of the space? Will this be adequate for your son Michael?"

Virgil struggled to get a grip on his emotions. Perhaps a quarter tab of Solo had been too much. He was feeling so expansive, so powerfully strong.

Ordinarily, he abided by the drug dealer's cardinal rule: *Don't get high off your own supply.*

But the stress of moving his operation from the safety of Sainte-Anne to the heart of Montreal was eating at him. He'd had to do something to regain his composure. But, as the tingling in his fingers increased to a jolt and the buzz in his brain reached full crescendo, he realized the Solo had been a mistake.

She was watching him with fearful eyes. He prayed she didn't have a panic alarm somewhere on her person. Because if she did, he suspected she'd be summoning help at any moment.

"Yes, yes. I think it will do quite nicely."

"And your Michael is a student?"

"Yes, at the University of Montreal."

He had to make it through this interview.

Although he wished he could find a place with the privacy of the old Lavoire Mansion, the reality was he didn't have time to look for the ideal spot. The apartment would work just fine.

Locating his illicit production center in Montreal was undeniably risky. There were too many people from his old life to run into near McAllen. And too many dealers from his new life to run into near Mount Royal Park.

Côte-des-Neiges was the best he could do to mitigate the danger. The densely populated central neighborhood was perhaps the most ethnically diverse in all of Canada—neither English nor French was the majority language. Between the various immigrant clusters and the transient university students, he thought he would find anonymity. And, in the event someone encountered one of his workers, he or she would likely assume the uncommunicative person was merely someone who didn't speak their language.

Yes, Côte-des-Neiges would work just fine. The sterile, charmless apartment would work just fine.

Another hysterical laugh bubbled up in his throat. He surged with power, and he wanted to fling his arms wide and declare himself master of all he surveyed. Instead he bit down hard on the inside of his cheek, until he tasted coppery blood.

"Shall we sign the papers?" he suggested in a strangled voice.

"Oh, monsieur, I'm so sorry. We will need to run the credit check first." Her voice was mournful.

He exhaled slowly through flared nostrils. "I think not."

She opened her expertly lipsticked mouth to protest. The words died in her throat when he pulled out his billfold.

He peeled off a dozen one-hundred-dollar bills. "Here's the deposit."

Another dozen followed. "And the first month's rent."

Her eyes followed the bills as they fluttered to the kitchen counter.

"What do you think would be a fair thank you gift

for your assistance in expediting this process for me, Ms. Wells? Another twelve hundred?"

"Oh, no, sir ... Oh, I couldn't."

"Couldn't you though? It would be such a help if Michael and his friends could move in early—this weekend."

He added twelve bills to the pile.

Her eyes flicked between the counter and his face. "Well, yes ... I suppose I could see to that."

"I'd be most grateful." He smiled. He hoped his grin wasn't too toothy.

She scooped the money into her pocketbook and pressed a ring of keys into his hands. "The silver one is for the lobby door. The larger gold one opens the apartment; and, of course, the tiny one is for the mailbox. If your son would just stop by the leasing office on Monday to register his name and get his building identification, that would be very good."

"Excellent." He'd work with Mike until the kid could master that task.

Now that he had the keys, he was desperate to be rid of her. After all, he *did* have an illegally parked van full of street drugs and dead-eyed zombies down by the river to attend to. The image of himself forcing her out of the apartment sprang into his mind in glorious technicolor. He gritted his teeth and steeled himself to resist it.

She started toward the door. "Shall we walk out together?"

"I need to measure ... for curtains," he managed through clenched teeth. "Good day."

She threw a bewildered look at the windows, which were covered with perfectly serviceable blinds. The she fled out into the hall. He listened until he heard the elevator bell and then counted to twenty.

When he was sure she'd left, he opened the door and ran down the stairs and out onto the street as quickly as he could.

By the time he reached the van, he was panting hard. He rested one hand against the van and caught his breath. Then he plucked the parking ticket off his windshield and muttered a few oaths. He unlocked then lifted the handles to open the back doors of the van and looked inside.

Three workers looked back at him vacantly.

The case of drugs rested on the floor where he'd left it.

Mike was gone.

# CHAPTER TWENTY-FIVE

**E**liza was still flushed with pride when the Black Swan panel wrapped up. She'd presented her findings without passing out, throwing up, or forgetting every word. Bodhi's smiling countenance beside her had been her touchstone for the first few minutes. But to her surprise, she'd hit her stride pretty early in her talk.

The entire panel had been well-received. Felix had proved to be a genuinely funny moderator. Some of his jokes had left the audience breathless with laughter. And the group had peppered all the panelists with a barrage of thought-provoking, well-reasoned questions and comments.

"I'd say that was a success, yes?" Claude Ripple said, giving Felix an enthusiastic handshake.

"Quite, quite," Felix agreed.

Seizing on the bonhomie and borderline giddiness, Jon announced to the group, "I say we skip 'Developments in Computer-Generated Modeling of Skin Necrotization Rates' and toast ourselves at the bar."

"I'm in," Claude said instantly.

"I suppose I could have a gimlet," Felix mused.

The idea sounded like a good one to Eliza. She was enjoying the camaraderie. And skin necrosis didn't hold a great deal of appeal.

But if they were planning to look into Tatiana's background, perhaps they should beg off? She threw Bodhi a questioning look.

"That sounds great," he said to Jon.

"Sure thing," Eliza chimed in.

As the group floated toward the exit, Bodhi caught up with Eliza and whispered near her ear, "Maybe we can try to get a little more detail out of Felix about the psych experiment Tatiana took part in."

She nodded her agreement, although she suspected Felix had already told them all he knew. He didn't seem like the type to hold back the good parts of a story. Or the boring parts. Or any parts, for that matter.

Two gimlets later, Felix was regaling her with a story about a cross-border body broker who trafficked in severed heads. She smiled grimly and sipped her mimosa.

On the other side of the table, Bodhi nursed his beer and made a chopping motion with his hand across his neck when Felix wasn't looking. She wasn't sure whether he was acting out the decapitations or signaling that it was time to cut short the drinks.

Then a medical school memory popped into her mind, and she realized Bodhi must've been miming decapitation, not signaling that it was time to abort their fact-finding mission.

She'd briefly shared an apartment with a woman whom Bodhi had nicknamed 'The Talker.' Olivia made Felix look terse; she somehow managed to stretch a two-minute story into a twenty-minute monologue. Out of desperation, Eliza and Bodhi had developed a code to signal that one of them needed to be extricated from one of Olivia's epic tales. The captive would raise his or her hands then cross them at the wrists and make a quick 'X' motion. Olivia had never seemed to catch on.

Eliza laughed softly at the recollection.

"What are you thinking about?" Bodhi asked in a low voice.

Startled, she met his eyes. "Olivia—that woman I lived with during our second year."

"The Talker." His voice was warm with amusement.

They smiled at each other, savoring the shared moment.

Then Jon said something to Claude that made Eliza's ears perk up and thoughts of their private joke vanish from her mind.

"I'm sorry. Could you say that again?" she leaned across the table and interrupted Jon.

Jon blinked at her. "Uh, I was just telling Claude that my office might have made a breakthrough in identifying that designer drug plaguing our provinces."

"Did you say it contains saxitoxin?" Her voice shook with excitement.

"Yes. It's a—"

"It's a paralytic shellfish poison. A thousand times more toxic than sarin nerve gas. I think the lethal dose for humans is somewhere in the 0.2 milligram range," she said.

"That's right," he said slowly.

"Don't look so surprised, Jon. There are no flies on the lady from Louisiana," Felix told him.

Claude roared with laughter. Jon's ears turned pink, and Eliza took pity on him. "I only know because an oyster farm in my parish had an outbreak of STX back in 2015. I autopsied a pregnant twenty-four-year old who died from paralytic shellfish poison. Callie Jackson," she finished in a soft voice.

The silence that descended on the table was laden with understanding. Bodhi squeezed her hand.

After a moment, she cleared her throat. "Immediately after consuming the oysters, she complained that her lips and face were tingling. By the time she presented at a walk-in clinic, her boyfriend was carrying her because her limbs were stiff and she was unable to coordinate her movement. She had a rapid pulse and heart rate and difficulty breathing. Within minutes of arrival, she experienced respiratory paralysis. It just happened too fast. There was no time to get her on a ventilator."

Jon made a sympathetic noise in the back of his throat. Claude studied his drink.

"Taking a recreational drug that contains saxitoxin seems an awful lot like playing Russian roulette. And I'm not sure what the payoff is. Feeling tingly?" Bodhi posited.

"These folks aren't just gambling with STX. We think this drug combines it with TTX and CDX," Jon said in bleak voice.

"Tetrodoxin—puffer fish poison? That one's a thousand times more toxic than cyanide. And very similar to saxitoxin. Tingling, numbness, eventual paralysis. And to answer Bodhi's question, people who eat fugu *are* seeking that tingle. But I'm told it also comes with a peaceful, light-headed feeling," Felix said.

"So this drug of yours contains two sodium channel

blockers and a snake venom," Bodhi mused. "CDX or candotoxin is also a neurotoxin that produces numbness, tingling, and can result in respiratory paralysis but it's also said to enhance sensation. Cobra venom pills are big on the party scene in parts of India and Southeast Asia."

"If we're right, someone's selling a drug that makes people feel electrified, which is probably a pretty big rush," Claude noted. "And in trace quantities, the effects would be temporary. But controlling the dosage of any one of the three—let alone all three together, not to mention whatever filler ingredients are used—has got to be impossible."

"Hence, your overdose epidemic," Eliza noted.

"I never thought I'd say this, but fatal overdosing is probably better than the alternative outcome—prolonged coma. With all that damage to the glia, combined with the suppression of the sodium channels, I imagine a non-fatal overdose would leave the user a zombie, for lack of a better word."

Eliza met Bodhi's eyes across the table. They knew a zombie.

# CHAPTER TWENTY-SIX

**B**odhi tracked down Guillaume Loomis in between sessions. He found him in the business center, helping a speaker print a slide presentation that had been requested by audience members as a handout.

"Could I interrupt for just a moment?" Bodhi tilted his head toward a small room in the back of the center that was set up for guests to make and receive private phone calls.

"Of course." Guillaume waved over a young woman wearing a hotel uniform and handed off the doctor and his printouts. "Please have fifty copies of this made for Dr. Borlotta."

Then he followed Bodhi into the telephone room. "I heard the panel was a smash. But I suspect that's not what this is about, is it?" He tapped his foot nervously.

"The talk *was* well-received. But you're right; that's not what this is about. After our presentation, the four of us and Felix had a drink together. Jon Malvern's lab in Montreal has isolated three components of some new street drug that's been causing a lot overdoses."

"Ah, yes. Solo."

"I beg your pardon?"

"The name of the drug is Solo—at least according to the Quebec City police, but they haven't confiscated any samples yet."

Bodhi blinked. "It sounds like they should coordinate with their colleagues in Montreal and Toronto. Jon and Claude say the authorities there don't know what the drug is."

Guillaume frowned. "Typical lack of information sharing. I'll talk to Inspector Commaire. So, Malvern has a sample?"

"No. They were stymied, so the toxicologist asked him to culture some glial cells. They ran a battery of tests on the cultures. She's certain the drug contains at least three potent neurotoxins—tetrodoxin, saxitoxin, and candotoxin."

Guillaume let out a long, low whistle. "Nasty stuff."

"Very," Bodhi agreed. "Nasty stuff that could paralyze a person, cause them to cease breathing and arrest brain function—at least temporarily."

Guillaume stared at him. "You think Tatiana Viant took Solo?"

"I think she may have. And I think whoever gave it to her knew she wasn't really dead."

"And the corpses in Sainte-Anne?"

"I'd test their hair and tissue for the trio of neurotoxins if I were you."

"Hot damn!" Guillaume fumbled for his cell phone.

"Before you call, I want to tell you that I know you didn't want everyone involved. I understand your concerns about bureaucratic wrangling and infighting. Believe me. But if you want me and Eliza to help you, we need to be able to share information with Jon, Claude, and Felix. Jon and Felix each hold a piece of this puzzle. And Claude has access to any information that comes out of Toronto."

Guillaume scrunched up his nose as if he smelled something unpleasant. He bobbed his head from side to side, engaged in some internal debate. He sighed.

Bodhi stared at him impassively.

"Fine. Yes, of course. But I must insist that you and Dr. Rollins are in charge. You're the consultants we've asked to look into this. You have to make that clear to the Montreal and Toronto labs, as well as to Felix and the folks at McAllen. You two are running a multi-province, multi-agency investigation at the behest of the Quebec

City police and coroner. After all, Tatiana Viant is here."
Guillaume laid out his conditions in a voice that
suggested the entire idea pained him.

"That's fair. We'll do that."

"Thank you." His shoulders sagged—whether from
relief or disappointment, Bodhi couldn't tell.

"One more thing."

"Yes?"

"As much as we hate to miss any of the presenta-
tions, Eliza and I are going to go to Montreal with Felix
and Jon this afternoon. After that, we'll see whether we
can attend the rest of the symposium, but—"

"Please. Don't concern yourself with the programming. It sounds like the two of you—the five of you—are
making progress. Do what you need to do. I'll tell the
inspector to have Officers McLord and Dixon contact
you directly with any status updates. If we can get a
handle on this drug problem and pinpoint a cause of
death for the four new bodies ... *mon Dieu*, it will be
nothing short of a miracle." He managed a brittle smile.

*A miracle.*

As Bodhi left the business center, Guillaume's final
words rang in his ears like a prayer or a chant.

# CHAPTER TWENTY-SEVEN

*Plaza Côte-des-Neiges*

Virgil found Mike at the mall. He was standing, transfixed, outside a music store listening to some employees who were playing electric guitars and drums in what appeared to be an impromptu jam session. Virgil observed him for a moment. His head bobbed in time with the music and he clapped his hands. None of the shoppers passing by gave him a second look. He more or less fit in.

Virgil's high was long gone, but now his agitation and worry were fading away, too. He waited until the song ended then approached Mike. He placed a hand on the younger man's arm and said his name softly.

"Mike."

Mike turned to face him. He scrunched up his face

in concentration and studied Virgil. Then he said in a definite tone, "Dad."

Virgil almost corrected him but quickly realized that having Mike identify him as—and believe him to be—his father could be beneficial. So he just smiled.

"You like music, Mike?"

Mike nodded. It seemed to Virgil that his response time was speeding up, as if his processing rate was improving. This was both good, because it made him more useful, and bad, because he'd managed to get out of the van and wander into the mall. If he regained more abilities, he'd be much harder to control.

Virgil would have to devise a way to keep Mike corralled. But, at the moment, his priority was to get back to the van to retrieve the other workers and his supplies and get everyone and everything settled in the apartment. The undertaking overwhelmed him. He suddenly, deep in his bones, understood how single parents of young, helpless children must feel.

*Parents. Parents have to keep track of their children.*

"Come on, Mike."

He led Mike to the directory of stores and scanned the list. But nothing looked promising. He huffed out a breath. He imagined he could find what he needed online, but he needed it now. Then he spotted the mobile phone store on the other side of the promenade. It wasn't what he had in mind, but he'd make it work.

Twenty minutes and several hundred dollars later, he and Mike emerged with a bag laden with wearable GPS trackers. The features made them perfect for his needs. The small, thin rectangular devices clipped to the inside of a pocket or a waistband and would enable him to locate his workers through his mobile phone. He would have real-time access to their locations if they wandered off. He couldn't afford a repeat of the Tatiana situation, especially not in an urban environment.

Having a solution to his worst fear lifted his spirits. Losing Tatiana and having to leave Sainte-Anne were just setbacks, nothing more. Solo would continue to grow. And, one day, in the not-too-distant future, it would move from the back alleys and parking lots to the chain pharmacies and doctors' offices. He just had to stay the course he'd set.

He started humming a lighthearted piece—Gustav Holt's "Jupiter." Beside him, Mike began to hum along.

## CHAPTER TWENTY-EIGHT

After a lengthy and unnecessary debate about how many cars to take to Montreal—which Eliza finally put an end to by pointing out that the four of them planned to return to Chateau Frontenac that evening and the environment would thank them for carpooling—they said goodbye to Claude and piled into Jon's station wagon for the three-hour drive to Montreal.

Waving off Felix's insistence that he take the front passenger seat because he had the longest legs, Bodhi climbed into the back seat beside Eliza and situated himself. Assuming no traffic, they'd reach McAllen University sometime between two-thirty and three o'clock.

Bodhi was about to ask Felix to call ahead to arrange

a meeting with his colleague from the Department of Psychiatry when his own cell phone rang.

"It's McLord," he said to Eliza in a low voice.

She raised her eyebrows and gave him a hopeful look.

"Hello, this is Bodhi King."

"Dr. King, Officer McLord here. Inspector says you and Dr. Rollins are to receive regular updates. We've identified the bodies."

"All four of them?" In his surprise, Bodhi spoke much louder than he meant to, catching the attention of the men in the front seat. Felix twisted around to look at him, and Jon flicked him a curious glance in the rearview mirror.

"Yes. All four were students at McAllen. They went missing at various points in the past six months. The last one just two weeks ago. And the campus authorities say they've got another missing person. A Michael Raglan, last seen just four days ago. He went to Tam-Tams on Sunday and never returned."

"Tam-Tams?"

"Oh, sorry. It's a music festival of sorts. Every Sunday, young people flock to Mount Royal Park. There's a drum circle that gathers near a monument to George-Étienne Cartier. People dance, drum, sing ... and get high."

"And Michael went there to get high?" If so, that would fit with the working theory.

"It's not clear. Kid was something of loner. The kids in his dorm say he asked where to get weed but never showed up at any campus parties. He kept to himself. Do you want the names of the deceased? We're notifying their families now. All hell will break out here when these grieving parents show up."

"Yes, I do. But two things first—one, ask the families if any of them have heard of the drug called Solo. And two, Dr. Loomis was going to have the coroner test the bodies for a specific cocktail of neurotoxins. Please make sure they put a rush on those test results. If they come back positive, you should contact the Montreal police and have them sweep Mount Royal Park for Solo dealers."

"With all due respect, I can't tell the Montreal police what to do, Dr. King."

Bodhi tamped down his frustration. "You can *ask* them, though. Right?"

McLord mumbled something.

"Officer McLord, there's a chance that Tatiana Viant took Solo and it left her in a condition that can fairly be described as the walking dead. It may also be responsible for the uptick in overdose deaths. Surely you can work with your colleagues down the road to save some lives. Can't you?"

Beside him, Eliza suppressed a giggle at his lecturing tone. He shrugged. He didn't have time for niceties.

On the other end of the phone, McLord let loose some more mumbling. Then he said, "The dead were identified as Jessica Clapton, age eighteen, from Hamilton, Ontario; Javier Martinez, age twenty, from Montreal; George Laurent, age twenty, from Alberta; and Sheryl Tarlington, age nineteen, from all the way over in Winnipeg."

"They were all so young," Bodhi remarked after committing the names to memory.

"Yes," McLord agreed tersely.

"Thanks for the update."

Bodhi ended the call and turned to Eliza. "All four bodies were identified as McAllen University students. And there's a fifth student who just went missing over the weekend."

Her big eyes filled with worry. "Good Lord." Then her eyes went wide. "I should call Nurse Grace and see if Tatiana's test results are back. They should test her system for the neurotoxins, too."

"Good idea."

He leaned forward to talk to Felix while Eliza placed the call to the hospital.

"I was going to suggest you call your colleague who knew Tatiana's name and ask if she could meet with me and Eliza this afternoon. But, in light of the news about the four students, maybe we should interface with the campus public safety office first? Or maybe the provincial authorities?" He directed the last question to Jon. His stomach sank as he realized he was completely out of his depth as to the proper procedure under Canadian laws and regulations.

"I can help you navigate the thicket of university departmental politics. I'm afraid I can't speak to how the SPMV—the Montreal police—will react to your poking around without their authorization. Especially because they're not going to be happy to learn the bodies are in Quebec City. Jon, what are your thoughts?" Felix deferred to the forensic biologist.

"I think the metaphorical feces is headed for the fan. We might as well get out in front of it."

"Meaning?" Bodhi asked.

"Meaning dead McAllen students are a shared problem for the university and the city. Felix works for one, I work for the other. We should set you and Eliza up with interviews on campus and then the two of us will meet together with our institution heads and work out some ground rules." He shrugged helplessly. "It's our only chance at averting a mess."

"You're right." Felix sighed. He turned back to Bodhi. "Tell me who you want to talk to, and I'll make the requisite calls."

---

E veryone but Jon worked the phones for the remainder of the drive to Montreal.

By the time he brought the car to a stop in front of the counseling center, Eliza had gotten a full report on Tatiana's condition and ordered the screening tests for tetrodoxin, saxitoxin, and candotoxin. She'd also called Jon's co-worker Lucy on speakerphone to ask what treatment could be offered if Tatiana had been exposed to the unholy trinity of neurotoxins for a prolonged period of time. The toxicologist told her she was working furiously to create an antidote and would loop in Tatiana's care team at the hospital if she tested positive. Lucy went on to reassure the four of them that she hypothesized that even with supportive care only, Tatiana should eventually recover.

Bodhi had received an update from the Quebec City coroner's office through Guillaume. Toxicology testing on the four McAllen students was being expedited, and Guillaume promised to immediately pass the results on to Bodhi and Eliza, no matter what time of day or night they came back. He went on to explicitly say he would not ask whether Bodhi or Eliza shared them through any back channels. Bodhi decided to interpret this as implicit permission to tell Felix, Claude, and Jon anything they learned.

Felix, meanwhile had arranged for Dr. Harris, the psychiatry professor, to meet with Bodhi and Eliza at a coffee shop right next to the campus counseling center. After their unofficial chat, Bodhi and Eliza would walk next door for an official meeting with the director of the counseling center.

"Jon and I will swing back and pick you up no later than seven. Any questions?" Felix asked, before they got out of the car.

"Nope. Good luck, you two," Bodhi said.

"Same to you," Felix answered.

"I have a question," Eliza grumbled as they headed into the coffee shop. "Don't any of you men eat? We skipped lunch, and now it sounds like we're going to drive back to Quebec City without having dinner first? I can't work under these conditions."

"Come on. I'll buy you a muffin the size of your fist inside. The sugar rush should see you through the afternoon."

"You always were a sweet talker," she said over her shoulder as she waved at a woman who fit the description Felix had given them. Curly dark hair, red-framed glasses, and a smattering of freckles. "There's Dr. Harris."

# CHAPTER TWENTY-NINE

"Just tell me what you want to know. I've got one foot out the door—I've been offered a tenure track position at UBC in Nova Scotia. So truly, I've got no agenda and no loyalty to the powers that be." Dr. Victoria Harris said as soon as she sat down at the table with her chai latte.

Eliza nibbled her cranberry muffin and nodded encouragingly.

Bodhi blinked at her candor. "Uh, congratulations on the new position. We appreciate your willingness to talk to us."

"No problem."

"We understand you told Dr. Bechtel that you recognized Tatiana Viant's name."

"That's right." She sipped her latte.

"How did her name come up?"

She tossed her head back and laughed. Dark curls spilled over her face and she pushed them back.

"Sorry," she gasped when she could speak again. "It came up because Felix is the worst gossip in the building. He pulled me aside and whispered 'did you hear?' then proceeded to tell me all about Tatiana Viant rising from the dead to roam the countryside. How did it come up? That's rich."

Eliza glanced at Bodhi. He was frowning.

"I see," he said slowly. "And when Dr. Bechtel brought it up, you said ...."

"I said I remembered her because I did. My office-mate—that's right, seven years on faculty and I was sharing space like some teaching assistant or junior researcher—anyway, my officemate ran an experiment last year, and she was one of his subjects."

"How did you happen to remember that? I mean, surely she was only one of—what, dozens of students who participated in studies last year?" Bodhi asked.

Eliza tore off another chunk of her muffin. Bodhi was doing great. She'd jump in when her blood sugar had stabilized.

"More like hundreds. But I'm pretty sure she's the only one Virgil was in love with."

"Virgil?" Eliza choked down a bite.

"Virgil Lavoire. He was in the Masters of Science degree program."

"Wait. A graduate student was running psychiatric experiments—had he at least completed medical school?" Bodhi interjected.

"No. The masters program is a research-focused training program. Applicants admitted to the program come from an array of disciplines—some medical, but also anthropology, neuroscience, genetics. Virgil's background was in psychology with a focus on social anxiety disorders."

Eliza had a different question. "Did you say his last name is Lavoire?"

Victoria cocked her head. "I did."

"Remember that mausoleum in the cemetery in Sainte-Anne?" Eliza whispered to Bodhi.

He nodded. "Any idea where Mr. Lavoire was from?"

Victoria was watching them closely. "Sure. Everybody knew he was one of the Île d'Orléans Lavoires. It's not as if he'd let you forget it. He wanted to make sure everyone knew he came from money."

Eliza's heart thumped. Her skin grew hot as adrenaline flooded her body. There was no way this was a coincidence. The researcher who experimented on

Tatiana and reportedly loved her came from the abandoned town where they'd found her—and four bodies.

Bodhi put a calming hand on her forearm and asked Victoria, "I don't suppose you know which town?"

"I should clarify. His family was originally from the island. I don't know the name of the exact town—some old village that's not even there anymore. But he grew up right here in Montreal. And so did his parents, I think. The name dropping was just this thing he did. We all sort of pegged it as an effort to compensate for not having a medical degree. Self-aggrandization." She diagnosed her former colleague with an air of certainty.

Eliza shot Bodhi a look. This Virgil person was their guy.

"Where is he now?" she asked.

"No clue. Not in the city, I know that much. After his study was mothballed, he withdrew from the program and left town with his tail between his legs. He was disgraced. I'm sure he didn't land in another master's program. Nobody would write him a recommendation."

"What did he do to get himself kicked out of the program? We know the broad strokes from Felix but we're interested in the details," Bodhi explained.

"I don't know all the details. Here's what I know. He came up with a research idea to start a support group for

174

undergraduates struggling with social anxiety. The format was that the group would meet once a week in a safe place and practice socializing with one another. He'd work with them on tools they could use when they felt overwhelmed in the face of a social interaction. The research design wasn't exactly groundbreaking."

Eliza straightened her spine and pushed the muffin away. "Something doesn't have to be groundbreaking to help people."

Bodhi noted her icy tone with a raised eyebrow. She didn't care. Victoria Harris had no right to be derisive about struggles she knew nothing about.

"That's true," she conceded, unperturbed by Eliza's reaction. "And, in truth, it sounds like his group was helpful to several of the students—Tatiana included. Her demeanor seemed to change after she joined the group."

Eliza nodded. "Her parents noticed a difference, too. They thought maybe she'd started to date someone."

"Maybe. It wasn't Virgil though. I got the sense his infatuation was one-sided. When I saw them interacting, she treated him like a professor she really respected. She was grateful for his help. He, on the other hand, mooned over her like a schoolboy. It was unseemly."

"Did you say anything to anybody—a graduate studies supervisor, maybe?"

"I did, actually. He said he'd talk to Virgil. And he did. It was that conversation that led to the program being shut down. I'm not sure what Virgil told him, but the next week the social anxiety support group meetings ended."

"How did Virgil take it?" Bodhi asked.

Victoria scanned the small coffeehouse to make sure nobody was listening to them. She needn't have bothered, Eliza thought. Each soul under the age of thirty—including the barista and the guy working the bakery counter—had a phone in his or her hands, head bent, eyes glued to the screen, fingers swiping and scrolling.

"Frankly, better than the students did. They were blindsided by the move, and it threw some of them into a tailspin. They came trooping into the office and begged him to keep the group going informally."

"Did he?" Eliza asked. Her heart ached for the kids who'd finally started making breakthroughs and then lost their support network.

"Yes. And that's why he was finally asked to leave. That's just an egregious breach of ethics and protocol." She finished her drink and checked her watch. "Anything else I can tell you? I don't want to run out and leave you with unanswered questions, but I do have a class to teach on the other side of the campus in ten minutes."

"We won't hold you up," Bodhi promised. "But there is still one point I'm confused about. Felix said that part of the reason the program was shut down was the participants didn't understand it was experimental. From what you've told us about the group, any data he collected would almost certainly have come in the form of self-reported survey answers, right? How could they not have known?"

"Now that I don't know. I just know what his supervisor told me after Virgil was asked to leave."

"Can we talk to him—the supervisor?"

"I'm afraid not. He actually left not long after Virgil."

"Oh?" Eliza's ears pricked up. "Was it related?"

Victoria shrugged and stood up. As she slung her tote bag over her shoulder, she said, "I don't think so. I mean, his reputation took a hit within his department, too, but the announcement that went out said he was relocating to Ontario for personal reasons. I assume he ended up at the University of Toronto. Felix would know." She smiled brightly. "I hope I've been helpful, but I really do need to run."

Eliza and Bodhi rose from the table.

"You've been very helpful," Eliza said as she pumped the woman's hand. "Thank you."

"Good luck in British Columbia," Bodhi said. He shook her hand next.

"Thanks for the drink." She tossed her cup into the recycling bin and swept out of the shop in a hurry.

None of the students glanced up as the door opened then shut behind her.

Eliza carried her trash to the receptacle then turned to Bodhi. "On to the counseling center?"

"Assuming your snack will tide you over for another meeting, yes."

"I'll manage." She flashed him a smile.

They walked through the quiet shop. She took a last look at the crowd glued to their phones. "Talk about zombification," she said in an undertone.

CHAPTER THIRTY

———————

Virgil walked through the kitchen to check on his workers. Mike was using the press to punch out the pills, Mike squeezed and released the handle rhythmically, humming as he worked. After each press, he pinched the compressed tablet between his fingers and added it to a pile to his left. Next to him, the blonde girl, Serena, counted out groups of twenty pills, saying the numbers in a soft voice. She pushed each set of twenty along the counter until they reached Reuben, the exchange student from Israel, who bagged them and placed them in the box. When the box was full, Jimmy, from Kentucky, sealed the box and carried it to the hand trolley parked beside the front door.

They worked slowly, but that was okay. Virgil was happy to see them handling their discrete tasks. Aside from Mike, none of them exhibited much personality or showed much spark. But they followed his instructions and tried their best.

The new apartment made the assembly line seem less bleak. He chalked it up to the sun streaming through the big, clean windows and bright lights—two features the mansion had lacked. Maybe the return to Montreal would turn out to be a positive development.

His wristwatch beeped at him to let him know it was time to dose the crew. He walked into the bathroom and unlocked the refrigerated safe where he stored the Solo ingredients. He removed a case that held five preloaded syringes. He had been experimenting with different maintenance doses for his workers, based on their body weights and how they appeared to metabolize the concoction. The liquid formulation enabled him to make more refined adjustments so as to strike the best balance for each of their unique body chemistries.

He wished he could do the same for the buyers on the street, but it was simply not feasible. What he really needed was for his partner to complete work on the antidote. His idea was to sell each hit of Solo along with a dose of the antidote, just in case the buyer had a sensitivity and the amount proved to be too much. A fail-safe to ease his conscience.

After he injected the workers with their day's dose

of Solo, he lingered in the apartment long enough to confirm nobody had a bad reaction. Then he took Mike by the shoulders.

"Mike, you're in charge until I come back tomorrow."

"Yes, dad." Mike nodded then went back to squeezing the press.

Virgil stepped out into the hall and waited until he heard Mike *snick* the lock into place. As he started toward the elevator, the young mother from 11-B turned from opening her door with a baby balanced on her hip.

"Hi, Mr. Mann."

"Hello." He silently cursed the chatty leasing agent for telling everyone who he was.

"Your son and his roommates are so quiet," she went on. "They're great kids."

"Thanks." He smiled and hurried toward the elevator to forestall further conversation.

When he reached the street, he pulled out his telephone and dialed a number in Toronto. He waited for his partner's out of office message to play. Then he said, "Call me when you can, please. I'm interested in your progress on the antidote. With the police sniffing around, I've had to move my base of operations. I can't afford another overdose."

## CHAPTER THIRTY-ONE

The counseling center director had changed his mind about speaking to Eliza and Bodhi. He refused to even let them into the building. Charming, reasoning, threatening—nothing swayed him. So, Bodhi stood outside on the pavement and called Guillaume, who called Inspector Commaire, who called the director's boss. Even that game of Telephone hadn't helped.

While Bodhi and Eliza sat on a low retaining wall and waited for Felix and Jon to finish their meeting, Bodhi watched the university students roaming around with travel mugs filled with coffee and bags weighted down with books. The medical students were easy to pick out. Regardless of skin tone, they shared a waxy, unhealthy pallor—the inevitable by-product of long, sleepless nights under the glare of hospital lights.

"I can't believe we were ever that young," he mused as a couple strolled by holding hands.

"Really? I can't believe we're this old. It seems like just last month we were pooling our change to get the Sunday paper so we could lay in the grass in Frick Park and do the crossword puzzle," Eliza countered.

"Wonder if college kids do the crossword anymore?" He smiled at her.

"Sure, Grandpa. On their iPads."

They were still laughing when his phone rang. It was Officer McLord. And he explained why they'd been stonewalled.

"I hear McAllen won't talk to you and Dr. Rollins."

"That's right."

"Can't say I blame them. I'm sure the lawyers have muzzled them good. Two of those dead kids were in that social anxiety counseling group with Tatiana."

"Which two?"

"The two who've been dead for the longest—Javier Martinez and Sheryl Tarlington. They both disappeared less than a month after Tatiana died. Or didn't die. Or— you know what I mean."

"Do the other two have any connection to the counseling group?"

"Not that we've been able to determine. Campus

public safety just went dark on us, though. Wagons are being circled."

"Thanks for the head's up."

"Don't mention it, Doc."

Bodhi ended the call with McLord and added this new piece of information to the puzzle he was working out in his mind. They needed to find Virgil Lavoire's advisor. Now.

Jon's car pulled up and came to a stop.

Eliza hopped down from the wall. "Yeesh, I can see the black clouds over their heads from here. This is gonna be a fun three-hour drive."

"I imagine the city and the university are busy blaming one another for this disaster. It was probably an ugly meeting."

They got into the car, and Jon peeled out without greeting them. The tires squealed in protest.

"It went that well, eh?" Bodhi asked.

"Let's just hope the bar's still open when we get back to the hotel," Felix answered.

## CHAPTER THIRTY-TWO

*Wednesday evening*
*Chateau Frontenac*

The bar was, in fact, still open when Jon, Felix, Bodhi, and Eliza returned to the hotel. It was also full of mingling pathologists who had not spent their day driving back and forth on Canada's Autoroute 20. The bedraggled group took one look at the laughing crowd and turned to leave.

Claude and Guillaume waded through the crush of people toward them.

"No, no, don't go," Guillaume said. "You've got to fill us in. Find an out-of-the-way table. I'll flag down a waiter and get us a drink menu."

"And some snacks," Eliza called after him.

Bodhi shook his head. The woman had been a

bottomless pit in medical school. Apparently that hadn't changed.

Jon took charge and commandeered a table tucked away under a window. Claude pulled up two extra chairs, and they all crowded around.

Guillaume appeared, trailed by a waiter bearing a divided dish of olives, nuts, and vegetables. Eliza gestured for him to put the dish in front of her. He did so with a small, formal bow then took their drink orders.

"So?" Guillaume said.

Bodhi waited to see who would volunteer to summarize their mostly fruitless trip.

Eliza spoke first. "Well, first Bodhi and I met with Felix's friend. She spoke to us in an unofficial capacity, and she was very forthcoming, thank goodness. Because when we showed up for our official meeting with the director of the counseling center, he refused to see us."

"Refused?" Claude sputtered. "On what basis?"

"I can shed some light on this one. On advice of counsel, the university has decided to complete their own internal investigation first. As it turns out, two of the dead students were involved in the very same psychiatry department study that Tatiana Viant participated in. Obviously, that can't be explained away as coincidence," Felix explained.

Well, actually, Bodhi thought, it *could* be a coincidence. But he wouldn't bet a dollar on it. Not-knowing only went so far. A person couldn't abandon all rational thought.

"And as a result of the university's decision to lawyer up," Felix added, "my meeting at Jon's office went rather poorly."

Bodhi had to feel for the man. His employer wasn't acquitting itself very well.

Felix seemed to sense what he was thinking. "I have every confidence that once the university authorities complete their investigation, they'll be more than happy to share information with the Montreal police and forensics unit again."

"I have no doubt either," Jon agreed. "But the current stalemate makes my job that much harder. Dr. Kim is working in the dark. And the people who have flashlights are pointing them away."

"How frustrating," Claude murmured.

"Was Felix's friend able to give you anything useful?" Guillaume asked.

"Yes. She gave us loads," Eliza answered. "The researcher running the study was a man by the name of Virgil Lavoire. He seemed to have a certain disregard for the rules, and had hooked up with a graduate advisor who had an equally lackadaisical view of ethics."

Claude leaned in. "Oh? Perhaps you should speak with the advisor."

"We wish we could. Dr. Harris didn't know where he landed." Bodhi turned toward Felix. "In fact, we didn't even get a name. Do you happen to know the guy?"

The waiter arrived with a tray of drinks. Felix grabbed his gimlet and took a big gulp. "I have to say I can't imagine one of the advisors at McAllen doing anything untoward. But I'm not sure that this is the time to for me to involve myself any further than I already have. I trust you can understand the tenuous position I'm in." He cast an apologetic look around the table.

Jon threw Bodhi a 'can you believe this guy' look, but Claude rushed to his defense. "I understand completely. I think everyone at this table is intimately acquainted with the vagaries of university politics. You can't jeopardize your standing in your department to play sleuth. We have to trust the process."

"Trust the process while teenagers are dropping dead in the streets? Are you serious?" Jon's voice was as cold as the ice cube floating in his bourbon.

Bodhi drank his tonic water and watched the expressions on his colleagues' faces. Eliza was puzzled. Jon, outraged. Felix was scared. Claude was sympathetic. Guillaume's expression was unreadable.

But the conference organizer removed all doubt as to his position when he said, "I quite understand the spot you're in, Felix. But you should consider where your ultimate loyalty lies—with your department or with the people we all took an oath not to harm. At some point standing by silently becomes harmful."

On that grim note, five stiff drinks were lifted to mouths and drained. Bodhi took another sip of water.

# CHAPTER THIRTY-THREE

*Mont Royal Park*
*Wednesday night*

Virgil strolled along the walking path until he reached the fourth bench from the restrooms. He tried to ignore his racing pulse as he took a seat at the end of the bench and rested his Tim Hortons takeout bag on the seat beside him. This part never got easier. He couldn't wait until Mike was competent enough to take over the deliveries.

*Soon. Very soon.*

He scanned the path in both directions and spotted the dealer wearing the bright yellow ski cap two benches away. He stood and walked toward Christian, leaving the bag behind. The African stood and walked toward him. They crossed paths near a stand of trees and, as usual, didn't acknowledge one another.

Sweat beaded on Virgil's forehead. He kept his eyes locked on the Tim Hortons bag sitting on the bench the dealer had just vacated.

*It's almost over.*

He reached the bench and scooped up the bag. He risked a quick glance over his shoulder. Christian was halfway down the path to the parking lot. The bag of drugs was gone from the bench, no doubt secreted away under the other man's jacket. He gripped his bag tighter. He'd wait until he was back in the car to count the cash, not that there was really any need. Christian knew better than to rip him off.

He let out a long, shaky breath. Just then his phone chirped, loud and shrill in the still night. His heart jumped in his chest and he nearly lost his footing. He got a grip on his nerves and leaned against a tree to answer the call.

"Yes?"

"I got your message. Please don't call my work number."

"Then give me your cell number."

"Or you could wait until I call you, per our arrangement."

Virgil's temper flared at his partner's tone. But they both knew who held the power in their relationship, so he clenched his teeth. "Okay."

"Good. Now, to answer your question, I'm still perfecting the formula. How's the sample I gave you working?"

"It's okay, I guess. When I give it to Mike he can concentrate. But he gets ... touchy."

"He's living in a constant state of impairment, Virgil. You'd be touchy, too. Regardless, I'm tinkering with it to see if I can reduce the side effects."

"Thanks."

"Don't thank me yet. You have a problem."

Virgil's stomach lurched. He hadn't mentioned the Tatiana situation. But perhaps someone else had. "Oh?"

"The reason the authorities were poking around in Sainte-Anne is that two Americans are investigating you."

He didn't question the information. He knew his partner had sources all over the country. "Why would two Americans care what I do? Are they police officers?"

"Not exactly. But they know about Tatiana ... and the others."

He willed himself not to vomit as fear roiled inside him. "The others? My workers?"

"No, you dolt. The dead ones."

He rested his head against the tree's rough trunk and closed his eyes. "What am I going to do?" he whispered.

"Listen to me, carefully. I have a plan."

His eyes popped open and he listened hard.

# CHAPTER THIRTY-FOUR

*Chateau Frontenac*
*Thursday morning*

Eliza was studying the day's schedule, trying to decide between a forensic anthropology talk and a session about reconstructing skeletal fragments, when Claude Ripple came around the corner gray-faced and tense.

"Eliza, thank goodness I found you. Where's Bodhi?" Claude panted.

"I haven't seen him yet this morning. Are you okay?"

"No, I'm afraid I'm not. I have important information for you and Dr. King."

Eliza stashed the program in her handbag and guided him to a couch in the lobby. "I'll find Bodhi and bring him over here. Do you need a glass of water?"

"No, thank you. Please, just get him," he gasped. He loosened his tie.

Eliza darted through the crowd, hoping she'd find Bodhi before Claude had a heart attack or passed out.

Finally, she spotted him talking to Jon and a blonde woman whom she had yet to be introduced to.

"Excuse me," she said as she stepped up to their group. "Bodhi, may I speak to you for a moment?"

Bodhi and Jon both gave her curious looks, but Bodhi excused himself from the conversation.

"What's going on? Did the hospital call with Tatiana's test results?"

"No." She shook her head. "Something's wrong with Claude Ripple. He asked me to find you."

Bodhi looked worried as she led him to the couch where she'd left Claude.

The Canadian was sitting with his head between his knees. Bodhi rushed over and crouched in front of him. "Claude, do you need a doctor?"

He lifted his head and chuckled weakly. "Well, this would be the place to find one if I did, wouldn't it? No, I'm not ill. I'm sorry to have scared you, Eliza. I'm just, well, I'm in shock. I got a call from Toronto this morning. There's a young man in custody who's in the same condition as your Ms. Viant. The exact words were 'a vacant-eyed zombie.' However, he seems to be somewhat more communicative than the young woman. He was talking about this Virgil character you mentioned last night."

Eliza felt her eyes go wide. She tried to tamp down her rising excitement.

"This may be the breakthrough we need," Bodhi said.

"I thought so, too. My department asked if you two would be willing to fly out there with me right now to interview him. They can't hold him for very long, as he hasn't been charged with anything."

"You want to fly?"

"Yes, it's a long drive but a short flight—under two hours."

Bodhi looked at Eliza. She nodded vigorously.

"Of course," he said. "Let me just talk to Guillaume and—"

"No. I'm afraid I must ask you not to say anything to any of the others just yet." He ducked his head and gave them a sheepish smile. Jurisdictional issues. You understand?"

Eliza tried not to roll her eyes, but she couldn't quite manage to resist.

Bodhi shook his head and said in a resigned tone, "Fine. But we will be filling them in when we return, correct?"

"Of course," Claude assured him.

Eliza could tell from Bodhi's expression that going behind Guillaume and Inspector Commaire's backs didn't sit well with him. But she also knew he'd say their loyalty lay with truth, not the Quebec City Police Service.

Claude went on, "If you can get your passports and be ready to leave within the next twenty minutes, we can make an early flight out and be there before noon."

---

**B**odhi spent the better part of the brief flight from Quebec City to Toronto meditating. He welcomed the quiet and stillness that had been so elusive during the past several days of activity. He cleared his mind of theories and questions that were swirling in his brain, pushed away the infighting and jockeying for position that had dominated the conversations, and focused on the people, living, dead, and missing who were at the center of the brewing storm.

Tatiana Viant. Jessica Clapton. Javier Martinez. George Laurent. Sheryl Tarlington. Michael Raglan. He held each name in his mind and vowed to unearth their stories for their families.

After several minutes, his thoughts turned to Eliza. Her broad smile. Her brown eyes. Her sharp wit. Her impressive appetite. Then he grew more serious. He worried about her ability to weather their investigation on behalf of the Canadians. She was keeping the lid on her panic attacks, but at what personal cost?

*It's not your place to take care of her,* he reminded himself. *You forfeited that job thirteen years ago.*

She'd be offended at the suggestion that she couldn't handle herself, anyway. And she very clearly could. He just had to hope she'd take whatever self-care steps she needed to keep the strain and stress at bay.

He exhaled a long, slow breath. Guillaume. Jon. Felix. Claude. Brilliant colleagues. New friends. But their ambition and their instincts to protect their fiefdoms intruded on their relationships. They could be prickly and petty. The competition was like a poison, and he didn't want to drink it in.

He wished each of them well in turn, sending them thoughts of peace and cooperation. It was all he could do.

The flight attendant's voice crackled over the intercom and intruded on his sitting meditation. He opened his eyes and listened as she welcomed the passengers to Toronto, home of the CN Tower, the Blue Jays, and the Maple Leafs. She must not have been a basketball fan because she left the Raptors off the list.

He turned around and caught Eliza's eye. She

smiled and gave him a little wave. Beside her, Claude appeared to be dozing. Bodhi hoped the nap would do him well. His nervousness back at the hotel had been so extreme that Bodhi really had been worried about his heart.

As if he'd felt Bodhi's gaze, Claude opened his eyes and looked back at him. His expression was somewhere between fear and dread—no doubt at the thought of meeting a member of the walking dead. It drove a finger of ice in to Bodhi's heart.

Bodhi shook off the unease that tried to settle over him like a sweater and smiled at Claude. Claude nodded and arranged his features into a small smile of his own as the wheels of the plane touched down and rolled along the tarmac, bringing them ever closer to the poor soul who might be able to help them fill in the missing pieces of their puzzle.

# CHAPTER THIRTY-FIVE

*Silence Restaurant*
*Downtown Toronto, Ontario*

"I'm so sorry about the delay," Claude apologized for the fourth time as the cab driver weaved through the mid-day traffic.

"It's okay," Eliza assured him for the fourth time. After all, it wasn't Claude's fault that the Crown Attorney's Office had decreed the young man needed to be cleared by a medical team before he could speak to them. Truth be told, she thought it was a prudent idea.

"Thank you both for being so understanding. I know you'll enjoy this lunch spot while you wait," Claude promised.

"Won't you be joining us?" Bodhi asked.

"I'm afraid I need to handle quite a bit of paperwork

to facilitate your interview of this fellow. So I'm just going to have the driver drop you off. But you're in for a treat. Silence is a genuinely unique experience," he promised.

"It's certainly an unusual name for a restaurant," Eliza commented.

"Ah, yes. Well, all the servers and kitchen staff at Silence are deaf, you see."

"Completely deaf?" she asked.

"Yes. The menu includes the sign language words and phrases for the various menu items, as well as the signed alphabet. That's how you'll order and communicate with your waiter or waitress," Claude explained.

"That *is* unique," she agreed.

"It's the only restaurant of its kind in North America —and possibly the world. And the food's phenomenal. I'll be eager to hear what you think of it."

The cab driver caught Claude's eye in the rearview mirror. "Hey, mister, where do you want me to drop them. There's construction right in front of the restaurant, you know?"

"Ah, yes. Pull into the alley then."

The cabbie started to say something but stopped himself.

"Is something wrong?" Bodhi asked

"Eh ... it's just ... this neighborhood is kind of rough." he said in an apologetic voice.

Claude waved off the concern. "It's marginal, true. But it's midday. They'll be fine." He turned to Eliza and Bodhi. "In fact, call me when you ask for your check and I'll have an officer meet you and bring you to the forensics unit. He'll pick you up in the same side alley."

Eliza nodded. "Sounds good to me."

Claude lived in the city, after all. If he was confident they'd be safe, she supposed he'd know.

The cab driver shrugged to indicate the decision was out of his hands. A moment later, the car slowed and he pulled into a narrow alleyway, lined on both sides by block-long brick walls.

"The restaurant's just on the other end of the alley. Turn right and it'll be the first door on the right. It's a one-way street though, so we'll just drop you off and then back out of here. *Bon appetite,*" Claude said as they exited the cab.

Bodhi and Eliza watched the taxi cab reverse out of the alley and disappear onto the street before they turned and walked toward the other end. Dumpsters lined both sides of the alley, but it was otherwise unremarkable, as far as Eliza could tell. She'd seen sketchier alleyways in Belle Rue.

They reached the end of the alley and turned right. The commercial drag where the restaurant was located did seem to be somewhat questionable. The restaurant was next door to a marijuana dispensary and directly across the street from an adult video store and a pawnshop. A check-cashing store sat catercorner. And, as the cab driver had said, the street in front of the restaurant was dug up. A construction truck sat empty in the middle of the crater.

"Well, one way or the other, this is going to be an experience," she said under her breath.

Bodhi winked at her and opened the door with a flourish. "After you."

---

V irgil watched as the couple strolled along the alley as if it were the Champs-Elysées in Paris and not a gritty side street. After they disappeared around the corner, he turned to Mike.

"Did you see them?"

"Yes. Man and woman."

"That's right. Now, Mike, listen to Dad."

Mike pinned his eyes on Virgil and waited for instructions.

"The man and woman are going to eat lunch. You stay here. When they come back, they'll be walking toward you from there." Virgil pointed to the south end of the alley. Mike's eyes tracked the movement.

He waited a moment, so Mike could process the information. After the young man nodded, Virgil went on. "When they come near you, step out from behind this Dumpster and stop them."

Mike's brow creased. "Stop them?"

"They're bad people, Mike. It's important that you stop them. And it's okay to hurt them."

"Hurt them?"

"Yes. Or kill them."

Mike shook his head *no,* violently, from side to side.

Virgil took him by the shoulders. "Look at me, Mike. Yes. You should hurt them or kill them. If Dad says it's okay, it's okay."

Mike hesitated, but after a long moment, he said, "It's okay for Mike to kill them."

"That's right." Virgil smiled encouragingly. "Now, let's take your medicine."

Mike obediently opened his mouth. Virgil squeezed several drops of the antidote out of the dropper and watched the young man swallow them.

He'd kept a close eye on Mike during the drive from Montreal because timing of the dosage was crucial, and it would have been too early to dose him before they'd left. But by the time the American doctors finished their meal and came back through the alley, the medication would have taken full effect. They would run smack into an aggressive, hypersensitive zombie who'd been ordered to kill. If that didn't solve his problem, he didn't know what would.

# CHAPTER THIRTY-SIX

B odhi smiled as he watched Eliza pick up sign language with the same facility that she used to pick up new medical skills over a dozen years ago. By the time their soup came, she was conversing with their waiter as if she'd been signing her entire life.

"What's the grin for?" she asked, after Edmund, their friendly waiter, sprinkled freshly ground pepper over their bowls and disappeared into the kitchen.

"I'm just enjoying our lunch."

"Uh-huh."

"I am." He dipped his spoon into his autumn vegetable soup. "This place actually reminds me of a restaurant I went to in Barcelona once."

She arched an eyebrow. "You went to a restaurant in

Spain where everyone was deaf and you ordered using sign language?"

"Nope. I went to a restaurant in Spain where all the servers and hosts were blind and we ate in total darkness."

Her eyes went wide. "Really?"

"Yeah. It's called dark dining. It was a very interesting sensory experience. It did get a little messy, though." He laughed softly at the memory.

She grew serious. "I don't think I'd like that. It would make me uncomfortable not to know who was near me."

"That's a reasonable response."

"I'd be afraid I'd have a panic attack, alone in the dark." Her gaze fell to the tablecloth.

He seized the thread she'd left hanging. "Have you been feeling anxious?"

"You mean, like, when we were traipsing through a cemetery in the dark or when I was giving a talk about my paper?" Her tone was light.

"Either one."

"To be honest, presenting on the panel was more nerve-wracking for me."

"I could see that."

She raised her head sharply. "You could? But you're comfortable speaking in front of groups."

"I am. But I'm not super comfortable hanging out in

a graveyard, digging around in the dirt until I find a corpse. We all have our comfort zones."

She pursed her lips and tried not to smile. "I'm pretty sure public speaking is generally less stressful than graverobbing."

He pulled himself up in mock offense. "I wasn't robbing the graves—just disturbing them."

Edmund appeared with their entrees. Bodhi turned his attention to the carefully constructed vegetable lasagna. It was light and flavorful. Eliza seemed to enjoy her duck and poutine just as much.

They practiced signing each other's names while they ate. Time sped by like water flowing downstream.

Just like that, she was tucking into a bowl of ice cream, and he was calling Claude's cell phone. He left a message to let Claude know they were just about done.

Edmund returned with their check, and Eliza signed out several sentences thanking him for his excellent service and complimenting the chef. Bodhi tried to keep the pride he felt from appearing on his face—he had no right to be proud of an autonomous, adult woman, yet there was no denying it—he was.

Edmund seized her hands and kissed her on both cheeks in the European style. Then he turned to Bodhi and rapidly spelled a message that he couldn't quite catch.

He turned to Eliza. "I missed most of that. What did he say?"

She gave an embarrassed laugh. "He said you're a lucky man."

Edmund smiled broadly. Bodhi signed 'thank you' and tried to ignore the pang in his chest as he followed Eliza out of the restaurant and onto the sidewalk.

## CHAPTER THIRTY-SEVEN

Bodhi saw him first. They had walked about twenty-five feet into the alley, when Eliza stopped to pet a stray cat that came out of the shadows to wrap itself around her ankles.

"Oh, Bodhi, I think she might be pregnant—look at her belly." Eliza bent and scratched the cat behind its ears.

He turned back and was about to tell her the cat just appeared to be well-fed, probably by the waiters from Silence, when movement flashed in his peripheral vision. He followed the motion and found himself staring at a broad-shouldered, blank faced young man. In an instant, his mind processed the vacant eyes, shallow breathing, and clenched fists.

"Stay there," he warned Eliza without taking his eyes off the man.

"Bodhi ..." she trailed off.

He kept his attention on the looming menace. The man shuffled forward with a stiff-legged gait. His head swiveled as he looked from Bodhi to Eliza and then back to Bodhi. His lips were moving, but it took Bodhi several seconds to register his words.

"Mike can kill the bad man and woman. It's okay to kill."

The words caused a chill to race down Bodhi's spine. The man repeated them over and then again, as if they were a dark mantra.

"Mike." Bodhi infused the word with authority.

Mike froze mid-step and cocked his head.

"Michael Raglan? Is that your name?" Bodhi guessed.

"Mike Raglan." He nodded slowly. Up. Down.

"We're here to help you, Mike."

Mike's entire face wrinkled with concentration. Then he said, "No. Mike can kill." He started to advance again.

"Bodhi, be careful."

Without taking his eyes off the man in front of him, Bodhi said, "Eliza, go back to the restaurant. Call the police."

"I'll call Claude—"

"No. Call 9-1-1. Okay?" he struggled to keep his voice calm.

"I don't want to leave you here," she panted.

He didn't dare turn to look at her, but he knew what he'd see if he did. Her pupils would be dilated; her skin, flushed; and her breathing, shallow and rapid. She was losing control. And a full-blown panic attack was likely to get them both killed.

"Eliza, please."

The cat mewled.

"Take the cat inside with you. You have to protect it. It's pregnant, remember?"

"But what about you?" A sob tore from her throat.

His pulse ticked up. He had to get her to safety. Now.

"I'll be okay. Go ahead. Pick up the cat. Go into the restaurant. Call the police. Please." His words were urgent but soft.

Behind him, she took a deep, shuddering breath. Then he heard her shaky voice, "Here, kitty, kitty."

Bodhi knew she had turned to leave because Mike's eyes tracked her movements. He felt his body sag with relief. Once she was safely inside, he'd figure out a way to deal with an automaton programmed to kill.

Mike's attention locked on Eliza and he started to walk

right past Bodhi to follow her. Bodhi waited until they were standing parallel to one another, then he hip checked the younger man into a Dumpster. The Dumpster banged off the wall behind it, and metal screeched against brick.

Mike covered his ears and fell to his knees, keening.

*Hypersensitivity to aural stimuli.*

Bodhi ran to the Dumpster. He lifted the lid and slammed it down with a loud squeal and three tremendous clangs.

Mike kept his hands clamped over his ears and squeezed his eyes shut.

Bodhi raised the lid again and let it drop. Mike whimpered at the sound and rolled to his side, tucking himself into a fetal position.

Bodhi abandoned his noise-making and hurried to Mike's side. He crouched beside him and put his hands firmly on the young man's shoulders.

"Look at me, Mike."

He kept his eyes tightly shut.

"I'm going to help you."

Mike opened his eyes. "Kill you."

"I don't think so. Someone told you to do that, but that's not what Mike wants."

Something—a hint of emotion—flickered in his eyes.

"What does Mike want?" Bodhi thought back to

what McLord had said. The kid disappeared after going to a drum circle. "You like Tam-Tams? Drums?"

Mike blinked.

Bodhi thought he might actually be able to get through to the guy before the police came. Then three things happened.

First, he heard a loud noise as a door opened at the back of the restaurant. He turned in time to see Eliza reappear in the alley. She was definitely not having a panic attack. She held a large kitchen knife and was flanked by Edmund, who held a very pissed-off cat.

Second, as she shouted, "The police are on their way," the cat leapt from the waiter's arms and streaked across the alley, hissing. It made a loud, strangled crying sound that tore through the air.

Mike's face contorted with rage. He clambered to his feet and lunged for the cat but missed.

Third, two black-and-white police cars with their lights flashing screeched to a stop, one at each end of the alley. Officers jumped out, shouting for them to get down, lie on the ground, hands above their heads.

Fear splashed across Mike's face. Bodhi could see that the man couldn't process the orders. The police continued to shout.

Fearing that they'd shoot Mike for not complying, Bodhi threw himself at Mike's legs. The guy's knees buckled, and they both tumbled to the rough ground. As they hit the ground, Mike twisted his neck and sank his teeth into the fleshy web space between Bodhi's thumb and index finger.

A police officer ran down the alley, his feet pounding and tackled Mike.

"Don't hurt him," Bodhi said as the officer managed to handcuff the young man. "He's been drugged and doesn't understand what's going on."

The police officer jerked his head around to search Bodhi's face. "You mean he's on drugs. What's he doing, Solo?"

"I think he's been held against his will by a drug dealer. He's been drugged—and weaponized. He was programmed to kill us."

A skeptical look crossed the officer's face. "Really? By whom?"

"Virgil Lavoire," Eliza said as she crossed the alley and took Bodhi's injured hand gently in her own hands. She turned his palm over from side to side, inspecting the wound. "Nasty bite," she said.

"I'll live."

"Is he infected now?" the second police officer said nervously, his gun drawn and trained on Bodhi.

"No. It doesn't work that way," Bodhi assured him.

Edmund joined the group and began signing furiously. He finished by pointing at Mike and then the police.

"What's he want?" the officer worried about zombie infections asked as he holstered his weapon.

"He's spelling out letters. G-P-S," Eliza explained. "But I don't know why."

*GPS.* Bodhi let his gaze follow the trajectory of Edmund's finger, which pointed at the bottom of Mike's jeans.

*GPS.* Bodhi leaned forward and lifted the cuff. A small, black box was pinned to the inside of the pants.

"What's that?" the officer who'd handcuffed Mike asked.

"I believe that's a GPS tracker," Bodhi said. "The man who's controlling him must have wanted a way to monitor his location."

The police officers grinned at each other. "So we're not going to have to go looking for this dirtbag. If we keep this guy here long enough, he'll come to us."

"Most likely," Bodhi agreed. He signed *'thank you'* to Edmund.

Then he stood and the alley began to spin. The edges of his vision turned black. The darkness spread and ran inward to the center of his vision. And then, nothingness.

# CHAPTER THIRTY-EIGHT

*Friday morning*
*General Hospital, Toronto*

Bodhi winced as he regained consciousness and sunlight filtered in around his eyelids.

"I sort of thought I'd be the one to pass out." Eliza's low voice sounded near his ear.

He turned in the direction of the sound and opened his eyes. He instantly regretted it. The light made his temples throb.

"Hi," he croaked.

He raised his right hand to stroke her hair and stopped midway. His hand felt too heavy and clumsy. He stared at it. It was wrapped in heavy white bandages.

Eliza followed his eyes. "After Michael Raglan bit you, you fainted. At first, I thought it was from blood loss because you were bleeding pretty freely, but the docs here tested your blood. Virgil kept his captives on a maintenance dose of Solo. But Claude had given him the antidote before he attacked us, so you got a hit of both at once when Michael bit you."

His heart rate spiked. A monitor to the right of him started beeping wildly.

"Don't worry. You're okay. They put you in a light, medically induced coma until everything cleared your system. I'll bet you've got one helluva a headache, though."

"Now that you mention it, yeah."

She nodded. "Open up."

He did as she instructed and she held a large tumbler of ice water up to his mouth. He sucked it gratefully through the flexible straw.

"Thank you."

"No sweat. You saved my life. And probably Michael's. Maybe the cat's. And Edmund's. I figure I can give you some water."

"You might be overstating the situation."

She regarded him with somber eyes. "I don't think so."

After a moment, he looked away. "So tell me what happened with Virgil. Did you say he had captives? Plural? And how is Claude involved in any of this?"

She took a deep breath. "I'll give you the short version because the police are on their way to pick us up. You're being released in about an hour. We've got to give the authorities our statements so we can make the afternoon flight back to Quebec City. I want to get out of here."

He took a long look at her exhausted expression and wrinkled clothes. "Did you spend the night in that chair?"

"Yeah."

"Eliza—"

"Whatever. I've spent lots of nights sleeping in hospital chairs. At least nobody was waking me up to perform surgery in the wee hours."

He chuckled. "Point taken. So, the short version?"

"Virgil Lavoire, grandson of the Sainte-Anne Lavoires, did, in fact, eventually track Michael down. When he arrived in the alley, the police took him into custody."

"Did he talk?"

"Did he talk? They couldn't shut him up. He told them about an apartment in some central neighborhood in Montreal where he had Michael and three other people working in a Solo lab, making drugs. The Montreal police went there, and his story checked out. The captives are at McAllen, at the hospital now."

"He held them captive?"

"Yes, Tatiana, too. Basically, whenever someone appeared to overdose on Solo, he checked to see if they had really died or if they were just suffering from respiratory and central nervous system paralysis. If they were dead, he just left the body where it was. But if they were paralyzed, he dosed them with a crude antidote and took them back to Sainte-Anne. Some of them died anyway—the four college kids we found in the cemetery. He wasn't very good at guessing the correct dosages, at first. But eventually he got better at it, so Tatiana, Mike, and the four others just sort of floated along in a zombified state."

"Wait. He has no medical training. How did he create an antidote?"

"He didn't. His old graduate program advisor from Montreal was working with him." She paused and raised her eyebrows.

"Not Claude?"

"Claude."

They stared at each other for a long moment.

Then he said, "Where is he?"

"He turned around and got right back on a plane to Quebec City before we even placed our orders at lunch. By the time you were being bitten by a zombie, he was in the air. He hightailed it back to the hotel and told Guillaume some BS story about me having a family emergency back home. He said we left for the States early Thursday morning and asked him to let Guillaume know."

"That story wouldn't hang together long."

"It wouldn't have to. The conference ended after breakfast today. He thought we were lying dead in an alley. If his plan had worked, the Toronto police would have had some leg work to do to trace the steps of two dead doctors from the United States. It's not like anyone knew we were staying in Quebec City."

"Eventually, the airline—"

"Sure, eventually. But he'd have vanished by then. Virgil, too."

"That clever son-of-a—"

"He almost got away with it. But since you thought fast enough to wage an aural assault on Michael, we were saved from death by Dumpster noises, and Virgil was taken into custody. After he sold Claude out, I gave the police Inspector Commaire's number. He arranged for McLord and Dixon to quietly take Claude into custody while he was sitting in the back of the audience during the presentation of the Lifetime Achievement in Forensic Pathology Award."

Bodhi cocked his head. "There's an award for that?"

"Can you believe it? It's called the Golden Bone Saw."

"Of course it is," he deadpanned.

She started to giggle. Her giggle turned into chuckle, which turned into peals of laughter that left her breathless. When she was finished, she wiped her eyes, and said, "I'm going to step outside so you can get dressed. Let's be ready to blow this popsicle joint when the police show up, okay?"

"Believe me, I don't want to stay here a minute longer than I need to. Beat it already, so I can put my clothes on."

She stood and turned to leave. She paused at the door and said, "You know, Edmund was right about something."

"What's that?"

"You *are* a lucky man. You're lucky you're not dead."

He waved her out of the room.

He shed the hospital gown and put on his shirt and pants.

Her words rang in his ears. The prospect of his death held no particular sway over him. Eventually he would die. But when he was standing in that alley, he had been terrified that *she* would die.

# CHAPTER THIRTY-NINE

*Friday evening*
*Chateau Frontenac*

After Bodhi and Eliza finished giving the Quebec City authorities the same statements they'd given to the Toronto police before leaving town, Officer Dixon drove them back to the hotel and promised to send the statements to Montreal to save them from having to tell their story a third time.

The police officer shook each of their hands and thanked them for their assistance in his serious, law enforcement voice before ushering them out of the car.

Bodhi visualized himself climbing into bed and pulling up the covers as he walked into the hotel's grand lobby. His bones ached. His mind was fuzzy. His wound itched. A dull headache thumped behind his temples.

Beside him, Eliza looked drawn and pale. Her hands shook slightly. Dark smudges bloomed under her eyes. She leaned into him and yawned.

He was guiding her toward the elevator bank when Guillaume sprinted down the hall, calling their names. Eliza sighed deeply.

"I'll deal with him," he promised.

Guillaume skidded to a stop just feet away from them.

"Are you okay? Really okay?" His worried eyes took in the thick white bandage covering the back of Bodhi's right hand.

"We're fine. We're just very tired." Bodhi shot Guillaume his most piercing look.

"Of course, of course." He said fretfully. "And you both need to rest but—"

"Thanks for understanding." Bodhi punctuated his interruption by pressing the elevator call button.

"Please." Guillaume stepped in front them. "Please join me, Felix, and Jon for dinner. We've arranged for a private room. A simple dinner—with a vegan dish for you. It will be quiet and easy. Please. We're so concerned about you and just devastated about Claude."

The plaintive note in his voice would have swayed Bodhi under ordinary circumstances, but he wasn't willing to subject Eliza to a group dinner. To his surprise, Eliza gave Guillaume a wobbly smile.

"How thoughtful. As long as you'll understand if I don't stay very long, I'd love to join you," she said.

"Eliza, are you sure?"

"I'm sure they're reeling about Claude. I think we all need closure. And, most importantly, I'm starving. A prearranged dinner will get food into my belly faster than room service." She laughed.

It was a creaky laugh, but it was a laugh. The sound of it eased Bodhi's heart.

"It's decided then," he told Guillaume. "Let's get some food into this woman's belly."

Guillaume led them to a cozy room where a candlelit table with service for five was set up in front of a marble fireplace. A small fire glowed in the hearth. As he shut the door closing the room off from the main dining area, Jon and Felix leapt to their feet and rushed around the table to greet them.

After a flurry of handshakes and hugs, their little group assembled around the table. As soon as he was seated, Bodhi drained his water glass. The cool liquid soothed his dry, burning throat.

Felix refilled his glass from the pitcher in the center of the table. Eliza passed the rolls.

"That's white bean spread," Felix said, nodding

toward the small dish beside the bread basket. "Instead of butter."

Bodhi smeared some bean spread on his roll. His stomach growled in anticipation. Eliza wasn't the only who was starving. He'd been so lost in his thoughts, he'd lost touch with his body.

Guillaume cleared his throat, ready to launch into an introductory speech of some sort, but Jon beat him to the punch.

"What the devil happened? And how did Claude get mixed up in this?" he asked with no preamble.

Guillaume closed his mouth and sat back, apparently content with skipping the preliminaries to hear the answer to the day's burning question.

Eliza swallowed a bite of bread and started the story. "Claude lured us to Toronto so his partner in the Solo-dealing enterprise, Virgil Lavoire, could have us killed."

"Not Claude," Jon insisted.

"Well, it's not clear that he and Virgil Lavoire were equal partners in the drug business, but he knew all about it. The entire time the Ontario Forensic Pathology Service was trying to figure out what was killing drug users, Claude had the answer and was working on an antidote. But not for his employer, for Virgil," Bodhi explained.

"But why?" The question exploded from Felix with such force that even he looked surprised.

Bodhi gave Eliza a sidelong look. They hadn't been able to figure out just how much Felix knew. He wasn't sure how to broach the subject.

Eliza was less worried with taking a delicate approach. She leaned forward, "Well, Felix, as you knew but never told us, Claude used to work at McAllen."

Felix's eyes bugged out. "The subject never came up."

"It seems a strange omission," Bodhi responded. "The four of us were panelists together, but neither you nor Claude ever mentioned that you used to work together."

"We didn't work together," he protested. "I'm on faculty. I mainly teach. His work was much more clinical. He spent a lot of time at the hospital. Our paths rarely, if ever, crossed. And he left so suddenly. It seemed as though he was embarrassed about the circumstances of his departure. So I ... I suppose I thought it would be insensitive to mention his time at McAllen ..."

"What were the circumstances of his departure?" Guillaume asked with naked curiosity.

"I honestly don't know," Felix said. "But you have to believe me, I had no inkling Virgil was behind all this.

And I certainly never imagined Claude would be mixed up in it."

Jon interjected, "How did Claude get involved, anyway?"

"He'd been Virgil Lavoire's graduate studies advisor. Because Virgil had an interest in therapies to alleviate social anxiety disorders and Claude had a specialty in drug therapies for mental disorders, they paired up. So when Virgil had the idea to augment the support group with a drug that he thought might help them, he went to Claude," Bodhi explained.

"Surely Claude didn't help this man give an untested, unapproved drug to human subjects," Jon said.

"No, it doesn't appear he did. He also didn't report Virgil to the university or the authorities. He just turned a blind eye. Virgil managed to get the neurotoxins on his own," Eliza said.

"And he convinced these kids to take the drug? How?" Felix wondered.

A waiter entered the room with a tray of salads. Bodhi waited until he'd distributed the plates and ground pepper for those who wanted it.

When the door quietly shut again, Bodhi said, "He told them it was a vitamin C tablet and that there was some evidence that vitamin C boosts moods, with increased sociability being a side effect. Who's going to object to vitamin C?"

"Nobody," Guillaume answered darkly.

"But Claude didn't *only* turn a blind eye. When Tatiana died, Virgil panicked. He went to Claude and told him what he'd done," Eliza said. "Claude didn't call the police at that point either. Although what he *did* do probably saved Tatiana's life."

"How so?" Jon leaned forward.

"Claude was on-duty when Tatiana was brought in to the hospital. He saw to it that she was ventilated right away."

"How? That's not his area," Felix noted prissily.

"He forged an order. And then he got a list of the ingredients in the Solo pill from Virgil and started researching how to reverse the effects. When Tatiana's parents had her moved to the hospital outside Ottawa, he gave Virgil a prototype antidote and sent him up to Port Gray to revive her. She'd been declared dead by the time Virgil got there, so he took her from the funeral home," Eliza continued.

Jon's face was mottled with purple splotches. "Are you telling me the whole time Lucy and I have been working our butt off trying to figure out what this new mystery drug was, Claude *knew*? He knew exactly what was killing people and he didn't tell anybody? He had an antidote and he didn't tell anybody? That's as good as committing murder."

"He's in deep trouble," Guillaume agreed.

"What about this antidote? Does it really work?" Felix asked.

"Sort of." Bodhi said. He turned to Jon. "Claude has agreed to cooperate with the toxicologist in your office on the antidote she's developing. According to Claude, they're quite similar. He used the potassium channel blocker 4-aminopyridine and krait antivenom as his building blocks."

Jon nodded. "That does sound close to Lucy's formulation. She's concerned about the 4-AP, though. Apparently there are some test results that show it does reverse saxitoxin- and tetrodoxin-induced respiratory paralysis. But it made rodents excessively irritable, prone to startling, and hypersensitive to stimuli."

Bodhi glanced down at his bandaged hand. "Yeah, it seems to have the same effect on humans," he said dryly.

Guillaume winced.

"I, for one, have great confidence in Dr. Kim's abilities. And, say what you will about Claude's ethical and moral compass, but I think his assistance will be a great benefit to her efforts," Felix said.

Eliza flushed. Bodhi could see the anger building in

her shaking shoulders. He caught her eye and took a long breath, hoping she'd mirror him.

The door opened again. The waiter cleared the salads and brought in the pasta course. Before anyone picked up a fork, Eliza stood.

"If you'll all excuse me, I'm afraid I have to go to bed right now or I'm in danger of ending up face down in my bowl of pasta. Good night." She dropped her napkin on the table and fled the room.

Bodhi watched her go.

"Is she okay?" Felix asked.

"I think she's not ready to talk about Claude. I mean, he *did* help Virgil try to kill us."

# CHAPTER FORTY

*Saturday*

"You really don't need to take me. I can call a cab," Eliza repeated.

"I *want* to drive you to the airport. It might be another dozen years until I see you again," Bodhi explained.

"I hope not." She smiled. "Besides, I think we're stuck with each other now. Guillaume's going to hound us until we write up a paper about the zombification of young people through neurotoxin delivery."

"Why don't I come up with the title?" He winked to let her know he was joking. "Come on, give me your bag."

The truth was she wasn't quite ready to say goodbye. So, why was she fighting his offer?

She handed over her rollerboard bag. "Thanks."

While the valet brought the rental car around to the front of the hotel and helped Bodhi load her bag into the trunk, she turned to take a final look at the Chateau Frontenac's grand exterior. She wanted to remember its grandeur and glamour to balance out the despair and pain that Quebec City would always be associated with in her mind.

"All set?" Bodhi called.

She fixed the image in her mind then slid into the passenger seat of the waiting car. As he drove, she fixed another in her mind: that of his smiling face.

After a moment, she said, "I called Mrs. Viant before I checked out of my room. She said the antidote is already working. Tatiana was joking around this morning. It sounds like they'll be taking her home today."

He glanced away from the road. "I sure hope Mike and the others improve that quickly, too."

"Yeah. I hate Virgil Lavoire and Claude for what they did to those kids."

"I pity them."

She whipped her head toward him. "What? No!"

He nodded but didn't speak.

"Bodhi, how could you even say that?" she demanded.

"Pure evil doesn't really exist, does it? Virgil and

Claude hurt a lot of families. They're responsible for unimaginable death and sadness, there's no denying that." He paused. "Virgil started out trying to help people, though. I've never experienced crippling social anxiety. But I can imagine that it's painful and stressful."

"It is," she confirmed in a soft voice. Then she said, "What's Claude's excuse?"

He exhaled. "Claude got in over his head. He was trying to help a friend out. He shouldn't have. I don't think he deserves your hatred."

"But that doesn't mean—"

"Let me finish, okay? They were wrong. Wrong to experiment on those kids without their knowledge, let alone their consent. Wrong to try to cover the near-fatal doses. Wrong to sell Solo on the street. Wrong to enslave the victims to further their drug empire."

"Wrong to send Mike to try to kill us," she added acidly.

"That, too. That's a lot of wrongs, no question. But no living person is irredeemable. If Claude helps the research team perfect the antidote, that's redemption. And if Virgil's original idea is used to create a safe drug, under controlled conditions, that can ease people's pain, that's redemption. Is the world on balance better because of what he did? No, of course not. But maybe someday it will be. Jon said there's talk of using the basic chemical fingerprint of Solo to create a pain killer for cancer patients. That would be redemption."

Her gut churned. All the words she could think of to say sounded bitter and hateful in her mind. Finally, she said, "Maybe I'm not as forgiving as you are."

"Maybe you're not as flawed as I am."

Her mouth fell open. "What?"

"I hurt you. Did I intend to? No, but I did. And I knew I'd done so. How am I different from Virgil Lavoire?"

She stammered, "Well ... for one thing, you haven't killed anyone."

"I caused you pain."

She had no immediate response to that. He *had* caused her pain. That was an undeniable fact. Finally, she said, "But you're sorry. And maybe Claude is, too. But I haven't seen any evidence of remorse from Lavoire."

"You're right, I am sorry. My remorse doesn't change the quality of what you experience, though. Does it?"

She was glad his attention was on the road because this conversation was making her jittery. Her hands fluttered in her lap. He exited to the airport ramp and followed the signs for international departures.

"Does it?" he pressed.

"No."

The single word hung on the air.

He pulled over to the curb and turned on the flashers. "If I could undo what I did to you, Eliza, I would. But I can't. And Virgil Lavoire and Claude Ripple can't undo their actions. But all three of us can do better going forward."

She put her hand over his. "Listen, I'm not enlightened enough to forgive them. But I do forgive you. Truly."

His eyes crinkled and he smiled. "Thank you."

After a long moment, he hit the trunk release. "I don't want you to miss your flight," he said. Then he exited the car and met her on the curb with her bag.

She threw her arms around his neck and hugged him. One thing she'd never forgotten about Bodhi was how complete and enveloping his hugs were. After a moment, she kissed his cheek.

"Come visit me in Louisiana. Fred and I will show you the town."

"I'd like that. And I'd like to meet Fred."

She turned and headed into the terminal. She could feel his eyes on her back as the automatic doors closed behind her.

After checking in, she found a seat and pulled out her cell phone. Fred answered on the third ring.

"I'm checked in. My flight leaves in two hours," she told him.

"Good. I was afraid you might've taken off with that Buddhist fellow." His tone was jokey but she sensed the underlying worry.

"Never."

"Glad to hear it. I'll pick you up at the airport. Let's grab dinner on our way back to town and you can tell me all about how you and your pal averted the Canadian zombie apocalypse."

She laughed. "Sounds like a plan."

"Good. How's Cleo's Oyster House sound?"

The specter of paralytic shellfish poisoning loomed in her mind. She shuddered. "I've got a better idea. Let's grab a couple of burgers from the Judice Inn."

"See now, woman, that's why I love you. After a whole week eating fancy French food, you want a great big juicy burger. Get yourself home so I can show you just how much I love you. I've been lonely without you."

"I'm on my way," she promised.

# CHAPTER FORTY-ONE

*Sunday morning*
*Old Quebec*

The hotel seemed empty to Bodhi, which was curious. The pathologists had mainly departed, true. But they'd been quickly replaced by vacationing families, the first wave of marketing professionals arriving for a conference of their own, and, according to Tim the valet, a pair of celebrity lovebirds trailed by an entourage of staff and a gaggle of photographers.

Despite the bustle and activity, Bodhi felt an emptiness. He nodded a greeting to the concierge and walked through the grand doors out onto the plaza. A final walk through the old walled city might reconnect him to the place and its people.

He started by strolling along Dufferin Terrace. As he stood at the edge of the boardwalk and stared down at the river below, he realized that he was lonely. He hadn't experienced loneliness in many years. The emptiness was coming from within. He missed Eliza.

He allowed this startling fact to sink into his bones. Then he continued along the terrace until he reached the Promenade des Gouverneurs and climbed up to the Plains of Abraham. He followed a walking trail toward the fort, stopping at a park bench to sit and think.

It was natural to feel Eliza's absence. They had a history, after all—they'd been lovers years ago. And they'd just spent several days working closely together, under dangerous, adrenaline-producing circumstances. Was that all this was? Or was this yearning something more?

Holding that question in his mind, he resumed his walk, crossing the grassy plains and passing through the arched stone gate into the walled city at Porte Saint-Louis. As he wound his way through the narrow, history-steeped streets, his thoughts returned to Eliza.

She was happy. She had a partner in her police detective friend, and he was glad for that for her. He wished her happiness and peace. And yet ...

As he followed the city walls to the descent to Lower Town the truth settled in his heart. He desired what she had. Not with her, not anymore. But a true friend to walk through life with, to share a meal and a bed with.

After years of solitude and celibacy, he now sought, not enlightenment or peace, but connection. The feeling knocked him off-balance. It was, after all, a sea change.

He U-turned abruptly and dodged a stroller-pushing mother with an apologetic smile. He retraced his steps uphill and came to a stop in front of the grand facade of the Basilica-Cathedral of Notre Dame.

He stood back and stared up at the towering cross, not at all sure why he'd backtracked to the church. He considered stepping inside. He'd learned in his travels that, for him, a cathedral, a synagogue, or a mosque could stand in for a temple to the Buddha. It wasn't the building or the specific iconography on the walls that served as a balm to his soul, but the atmosphere of quiet contemplation.

He stepped forward and was jostled by a man hurrying past him.

"Excusez-moi, je suis désolé," the man murmured an apology in rapid French as he kept walking. He turned into a gate and entered a courtyard next door to the cathedral.

Bodhi read the sign posted on the gate's wall. The sprawling campus was home to the historic Quebec Seminary. A thought bloomed in his mind.

He turned away from the church and removed his phone from his pocket. He had a better idea than slipping into a church pew for a few minutes.

He dialed a number in rural Illinois and listened patiently as it rang three times.

"Roshi, this is Bodhi King. May I come and stay for a while?"

## THANK YOU!

Bodhi will be back in his next adventure soon! If you enjoyed this book, I'd love it if you'd help introduce others to the series.

*Share it.* Please lend your copy to a friend.

*Review it.* Consider posting a short review to help other readers decide whether they might enjoy it.

*Connect with me.* Stop by my Facebook page for book updates, cover reveals, pithy quotes about coffee, and general time-wasting.

*Sign up.* To be the first to know when I have a new release, sign up for my email newsletter at www.melissafmiller.com. I only send emails when I have book news —I promise.

While I'm busy writing the next book, if you haven't read my Sasha McCandless, my Aroostine Higgins series, or my We Sisters Three series, you might want to give them a try.

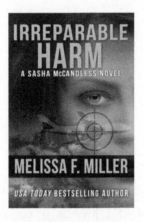

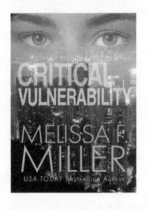

THANK YOU!

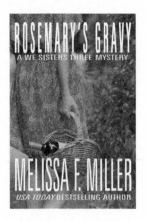

*USA Today* bestselling author Melissa F. Miller was born in Pittsburgh, Pennsylvania. Although life and love led her to Philadelphia, Baltimore, Washington, D.C., and, ultimately, South Central Pennsylvania, she secretly still considers Pittsburgh home.

In college, she majored in English literature with concentrations in creative writing poetry and medieval literature and was STUNNED, upon graduation, to learn that there's not exactly a job market for such a degree. After working as an editor for several years, she returned to school to earn a law degree. She was that annoying girl who loved class and always raised her hand. She practiced law for fifteen years, including a stint as a clerk for a federal judge, nearly a decade as an attorney at major international law firms, and several years running a two-person law firm with her lawyer husband.

Now, powered by coffee, she writes legal thrillers and homeschools her three children. When she's not writing, and sometimes when she is, Melissa travels around the country in an RV with her husband, her kids, and her cat.

*Connect with me*:

www.melissafmiller.com

## ACKNOWLEDGMENTS

Many thanks to everyone involved in the production of this book—in particular, my phenomenal editing and design team.